JUST

Clare Bevan was [...], where she still liv[...] [...]d cats. Previously a teacher, Clare has an Open University degree. Her main hobby is amateur dramatics, and she has written many plays, sketches and monologues. Her first novel, *Mightier than the Sword*, won the Kathleen Fidler Award, and is also available in Puffin.

Just Like
SUPERMAN

Clare Bevan

PUFFIN BOOKS

PUFFIN BOOKS

Published by the Penguin Group
Penguin Books Ltd, 27 Wrights Lane, London w8 5tz, England
Penguin Books USA Inc., 375 Hudson Street, New York, New York 10014, USA
Penguin Books Australia Ltd, Ringwood, Victoria, Australia
Penguin Books Canada Ltd, 10 Alcorn Avenue, Toronto, Ontario, Canada m4v 3b2
Penguin Books (NZ) Ltd, 182–190 Wairau Road, Auckland 10, New Zealand

Penguin Books Ltd, Registered Offices: Harmondsworth, Middlesex, England

First published by Blackie Children's Books 1992
Published in Puffin Books 1994
10 9 8 7 6 5 4 3 2 1

Printed in England by Clays Ltd, St Ives plc

CONTENTS

*Dedicated to Mum and Dad Smith, and Mum Bevan,
who know plenty of stories just like Gran's.
Also to Bill Whisker who was actually there.*

1
Goggles

I'm the weediest kid in our class and my glasses look like the bottoms of bottles. So, as you can see, I'm not exactly a Super Hero. What's more, my Dad's gone off to live somewhere else, and my Mum's a Fluffer.

Go on. Admit it. You don't know what a Fluffer is, do you? Mind you, I don't see why you should, unless your Mum happens to be a Fluffer too, which isn't very likely. Fluffing's one of those invisible jobs that just seem to get done by magic, like painting the stripes on zebra crossings. No one realizes it has to be done at all. But it does, and I'll tell you why.

All day long, people in London buy Underground tickets and stand around on Tube stations tapping their feet. And while they're waiting for their train to come along, they chew toffees or comb their hair or read papers to pass the time. After a while there's a whoosh of air along the tunnel, and they all start cramming together on the edge of the platform so they can grab a seat as soon as their train stops.

Now, most of them have been dropping litter. There's the obvious stuff like crisp bags and sweet wrappers and lumps of pink bubblegum, but there's plenty of not-so-obvious stuff too. Tiny grains of rubber off the soles of their shoes. Hair, loads of it, especially if anyone's started to go bald. And even flakes of skin. Disgusting, isn't it? Just think of that next time you scratch your head, or ping your sock-elastic in public.

Anyway, all that rubbish collects around the railway lines and makes heaps of fluff. Tons of it. And if someone didn't come along to clear it all up, there'd be power failures and breakdowns and all sorts of bother. So that's where my Mum comes in. Every night, when the last train goes off to the depot, she nips down the Underground with my Auntie Hat and a whole crowd of other women to clear all the rubbish and fluff out of the works. That's why they're called the Fluffers and that's how they earn their living.

Weird, isn't it? My Mum says it can be dead creepy when you first start. Lots of girls only stick it for about a week. Then they give up and get jobs in shops or flower markets instead. But my Mum likes the tunnels and the darkness. It takes all sorts, I suppose.

'It's nice and quiet down there,' she says. 'Gives you time to think. Time to sort out your worries. And you never know what treasures you might find, do you?'

Mostly, she just finds mice. I think they must live on stale crisps and apple cores, but perhaps they like being in the dark too. To tell you the truth, so do I. Even when I was very small I wouldn't ask for a torch or a nightlight at bedtime. The blackness always seemed cosy and friendly to me, like a big warm blanket covering my head. 'You can tell he comes from a family of Fluffers,' people used to say, and for some reason they always thought that was incredibly funny.

Mum generally comes home at about the time I get up, so we sit down and have our breakfast together, only she calls it tea. Then I go off to school and she goes off to have a long soak in the bath. You'd think she'd grumble about all the dust and the awkward hours, but she doesn't.

'I come from a long line of Fluffers,' she says. 'There's my big sister, Auntie Hat, of course. Then there's your

Gran. She worked down the tunnels before I was born. And there was my Gran as well, or so I'm told. So that's the way it is. I'm just a born Fluffer.'

'Well, I'm not,' says my sister Jackie. 'You'll never catch me in a pair of rotten dungarees. I'm going to be a fashion designer.'

Jackie's studying art and design at school, and she spends all her spare time drawing stringy women with such long legs they look like storks. They're everywhere. Our house is full of them. Pictures stuck to the fridge, doodles all over the telephone book, sketches on the toilet door. It's a wonder I don't have nightmares about stork-women in fluffy dungarees charging down tunnels and chasing giant mice. But the point is...what I'm trying to say...our house is hardly normal, is it? And I haven't even told you about my mad Gran yet. Still, maybe I'd better save her for later and get on with the story.

You see, the funniest thing of all is that I didn't even realize my life was unusual at the start. This was mainly because I hardly lived at home at all when I was little. I'd been born with a hole in my heart, so I was always very weak and spindly. For a long time I was in nursing homes, being fussed over and treated like a baby. Then I went to a special school where all the other kids had troubles of their own. Some of them couldn't walk, and some needed sticks to get around. Some of them looked OK on the outside, but they had to have medicines and exercises to keep them going.

Yet, although every one of us had something wrong, we felt we were normal. After all, we liked doing the same things as anyone else. Playing games, watching TV, eating chocolate, fooling about. So we started to think we'd all be cured by the time we grew up.

'When my heart's mended,' I used to say, 'I'm going to climb mountains and fight crocodiles with my bare

9

hands. I'm going to be a world famous pole vaulter. I'm going to swim the English Channel and win medals for bravery.'

Then one day it actually happened. Not the adventurous stuff. The heart operation. I found out afterwards that it had all been a bit touch-and-go, but when I came round, Mum was crying and Jackie had drawn me a Get Well card covered in stork-women, so I knew I was going to be all right.

As soon as I was well enough, I went back to school and Mum gave me a cake to share with all my old friends. The icing looked slightly grey and fluffy but no one dropped dead after eating it, so it can't have been too poisonous. The message on the top said 'Bon Voyage', and Mum had made a lucky black cat out of marzipan, which was a nice idea except that it tasted terrible.

That was my big turning point, and it took me completely by surprise. The next thing I knew, I was walking down the street past Mum's tube station, and in through the gates of our local primary school. That was when I finally discovered I was different.

'What's up with you then?' shouted the other boys. 'Why are you so skinny? Don't you know how to kick a football? Why are you always out of breath? What a wimp!'

'Goggles', they called me, and that was when they were being polite. I felt really lonely and miserable. I'd never had the chance to play proper team games before, so I was hopeless at all the things boys are supposed to do easily. I couldn't catch. I couldn't run fast. I couldn't swing a decent punch.

I'd read in a book that animals have a system called a pecking order. It works like this. The boss bird always gets the best food, the next bird gets the second best food, and so on down the list until the scraggiest bird gets nothing but scraps and grit. It's the same for pigs and cats and wolves.

Well, at my new school I was right at the bottom of the pecking order. The last one picked for the team, the last one to get a seat in the TV room, the last one to choose a library book, the last one in the dinner queue. Not that lunch-time mattered too much. In fact, I was quite glad to be slower than the others, because it meant I could help the dinner ladies finish up the chocolate pudding, or hang around stacking chairs instead of freezing in a corner of the playground.

After I'd been at the school for about a month, our teacher, Mr McAvity, told us to bring in our swimming gear, because it was our turn to visit the local baths. We were booked for a session every Thursday afternoon, and we were all going to start working towards our swimming certificates. This cheered me up a lot, although I couldn't tell anyone. There was no one to tell. The girls hardly ever spoke to me, and the boys weren't interested in anything I had to say. So I kept my feelings to myself.

That Thursday we all piled into the coach, and I sat in the only empty seat, next to McAvity. I could hear all the other kids behind me nattering and swapping funny stories, but I didn't say a word. Later, in the changing room, I waited for a space on the benches, and by the time I arrived at the pool everyone else was already splashing about or doing belly flops off the side.

I curled my toes over the cold rim of the tiles as the nurses had taught me, and stretched my arms high and straight. I'd always loved this part, just before take off, when I felt like a bird about to fly away to freedom. I was ready to jump when I realized everything had gone quiet.

'Gawd. Look at that,' gurgled one of the girls. 'He's

11

been sliced open. Looks like he's been attacked by tigers.'

I'd completely forgotten about my scars. They didn't bother me. They were just an ordinary part of life. One boy at my old school had been through so many operations on his legs that he looked like Frankenstein's monster from the knees down. So I didn't feel particularly special. In fact, it came as a surprise to find everyone staring at me.

'Look out,' I called. 'I'm diving in.' Then I shot over their wet heads to cut cleanly into the water.

When I surfaced, I shook my hair and started to sidestroke lazily across to McAvity, who was standing by the steps in a squelchy tracksuit. Swimming was my favourite sport. Well, let's face it. It was my only sport. While my heart had been bad, I hadn't been allowed much else, but there was a small pool in the school grounds and I'd been sent there most days for a spot of exercise to keep me fit.

'Splendid,' said McAvity. 'You appear to be something of a natural. You'd better go in the dolphin group.' He pointed at a row of children lined up beside a low diving board, so I shot off in their direction while the beginners made gasping noises behind me.

After the lesson, you'd have thought I was the most popular kid in the class. Everyone in the boys' changing room came stampeding over to talk to me, but Nig Coombes elbowed them out of the way. He was top of the pecking order all right. He had been sent out of the pool early for messing about, so he was the only person who was already dry and warm.

'What happened to you then?' he demanded. His voice sounded as if it had broken, but maybe it was just rough from too much smoking. We all knew he stole cigarettes from his Mum, and that she blamed his Dad whenever the supplies ran out.

I cleared my own throat, although there was nothing wrong with it. I needed the time. 'What?' I answered, as casually as I could. 'This scar, you mean?'

'Yeah,' said Nig.

'Yeah,' echoed the others, bobbing up and down behind him to get a better look at me.

I put on my glasses and blinked back at them. What was I going to say? For the very first time in my whole life I was being treated like a hero, and I didn't want to spoil everything straightaway. I shivered and wrapped my towel round my shoulders.

'Well,' said Nig. 'Tell us then.'

'Yeah,' said the others. 'Tell us then.'

OK...So what would you have done? Made up some story about being attacked by aliens from outer space, or being chased down a subway by a mad axe-man? They'd have guessed at once. I'm a hopeless liar.

On the other hand, I couldn't bear to tell them the boring old truth and spoil their day. I could see from their faces they thought I must be hiding some incredible mystery. Perhaps I had once been strong and athletic and fearless. Then disaster had struck, leaving me unconscious and bleeding to death in the gutter. But I had courageously fought my way back to life, and now here I was with a chest full of stitches to prove it. If I told them I'd always been a pathetic little squirt, and that my operation had actually made me stronger, they'd be really disappointed. So I started rubbing my head with my towel, to stall for time.

'Sorry,' I said through the damp stripes. 'Can't tell you the details. It's a family secret. See?'

They groaned, and most of them drifted away to dry themselves because they were getting chilly, standing around in their soggy trunks. But Nig hung about.

'Go on,' he said in a matey sort of way. 'You can tell me. How did it happen? A fight was it?'

13

I shrugged. I hoped I looked cool and careless, but really I was just praying he'd go away and leave me alone. 'Just one of those things,' I muttered into my sports bag. His shadow made me nervous.

He lifted up his hand with a quick movement, and for a moment I thought he was going to swipe me round the head, but then I saw he was tapping the side of his nose. He didn't say anything, but the look in his eyes meant, 'I understand, mate. Your secret's safe with me.'

Back at the coach, a space had miraculously appeared on the back seat. I don't know how, because no one was sitting next to McAvity, and we hadn't lost anyone down the plug-hole.

'Over here, Goggles,' called Nig. 'Make yourself at home.'

I squashed into the gap between him and the Parker twins, Nosy and Pam. It was a terrible ride. Nig kept telling me jokes I couldn't understand, and nudging me in the ribs to make me laugh in the right places. And Pam kept wringing her hair out over my jacket. By the time we got to the school gates, I felt like death warmed up. I'd probably overdone it a bit in the swimming pool. My body still wasn't used to normal amounts of exercise, though I was getting fitter every day thanks to the chair-lifting sessions at lunch-time. All the same, I nearly keeled over when I climbed down the steps, and Pam had to hold my bag for me while I got my breath back. I was shivering all over, and the wet jacket had stuck to my shirt.

'Don't worry, Sir,' said Nig to McAvity. 'We'll walk him home. Won't we, Nosy?'

'Yeah,' said the Parker twins. They did most things together, and they were both in the school swimming team, but apart from that you wouldn't have guessed they came from the same planet. Nosy was thin and shifty, with fair hair that flopped in his eyes. Pam was built like an American football player, and her hair looked like rusty barbed wire. One of her front teeth was cracked, and she could whistle so loud you thought your ears would explode.

She slung my bag across her shoulders and took my elbow in her hand with a grip like a monkey wrench. Nosy took my other elbow, the wet one, and they frog-marched me away down the road after Nig. There was certainly no chance that I was going to collapse or roll under a bus. I was home before I had time to panic, and dumped on my doorstep like a human milk bottle, only paler.

Mum was still in bed, but Gran made mother-hen noises when she saw me and soon warmed me up with a bowl of tinned soup, while I sat in the armchair scratching my scar and wondering if the whole world had gone crazy.

Maybe it had, because I was the local hero for the rest of that week. Little first years would come up and ask me if they could look at my wounds, then stagger away again pretending to feel sick. People made room for me in queues and whispered about me behind their hands. One of the girls, a drippy kid called DD, even took to following me around like a private fan club.

When Nig wasn't playing five-a-side or wrestling, he would show me off like a rare animal at the zoo. 'Meet Goggles. And don't be fooled. He's a lot tougher than he looks.' This was always accompanied by much winking and nose-tapping, although I don't think anyone understood what he was getting at. I didn't either. I mean, he didn't really know anything about me, did he? So how could he tell anyone else?

All the same, the rumours began. By Friday afternoon I was the sole survivor of an air crash; I'd been a human cannon ball, and I'd fought off a mad bull at a picnic.

I'd fallen through a plate glass window for a dare; I'd been buried alive in an earthquake, and I'd been savaged by a lioness at Windsor Safari Park. I'd also been crushed by a church spire during the last hurricane. You name it, I'd done it. No wonder I was treated like a celebrity. I'm surprised no one wanted my autograph.

'You can join our gang if you like,' said Nig after school. 'Tomorrow morning, ten o'clock. The old garages round the back of my house. Don't tell anyone.'

'Right,' I said, trying to sound excited. I didn't much fancy spending my weekend with a crowd of thugs like Nig, but I wasn't daft enough to say so. 'I'll see if my Mum'll let me.'

'Let you?' Nig snorted. 'Don't ask her, then. Just be there.'

'Right,' I said feebly.

There was no problem, anyway. Mum seemed only too glad to get me out of the house for a change. 'Have a nice time,' she said as I pulled on my jacket. 'Don't forget to wear your scarf. It's a bit blowy out there today.' She tucked me up so warmly I could hardly move my head, then crammed a clean handkerchief in my pocket. 'Don't be late. Supper's at one.' By which she meant lunch, of course.

Then she opened the front door and bundled me outside into the street. Gran was nodding and waving at me from behind the curtains, so I waved back as cheerfully as I could before I trudged off to find the garages.

2
The Garage Gang

Nig's house was one of those terraced places with a patch of trampled earth for a front garden, and a buckled bike rotting by the steps. Two doors along there was an alley-way. It wasn't exactly inviting. It smelt of tom cats and the walls were spattered with spray-on swear words, but I didn't have much choice. There wasn't anywhere else to go.

I plodded along it at my normal speed, about two miles a fortnight, and tried not to breathe until I came out into the fresh air again, if you could call it fresh. Apart from the whiff of dustbins, it was heavy with smoke. Not the rich, foody smoke of bonfires and barbecues. This was the scratchy, choking smell of cheap cigarettes, so I knew I must be on the right track.

In front of me stood a row of concrete garages. Most were locked or held shut with wire. One had a broken door, and inside I could see a stack of dented paint tins next to a deep freezer with green stuff growing round the lid.

'Nig!' I called. My voice sounded so jumpy it was embarrassing. 'Are you there?'

By way of an answer, I heard a burst of rude laughter coming from the end garage. It was Nig's gang all right. I'd have recognized Pam's hooting anywhere. I edged across and knocked on the metal door. The corrugated iron rattled.

17

'Who is it?' bellowed Nig. 'Push off, or we'll bung you in the bottle bank.'

More laughter from Pam.

'It's me,' I piped. 'Goggles. You told me to come. Remember?'

The door opened, I was dragged inside, and the door clanged shut again behind me.

I thought I was going to suffocate at first. My eyes were stinging so much, I had to take off my glasses and rub them on my sleeve.

'Hello Nig,' I spluttered. 'Not late am I?'

'Nah,' said Nig. 'Sit down. Have a ciggy.'

I sat on an upturned box someone had shoved underneath me, and looked around. The only light came from the holes in the roof, and a torch which dangled from the cross-beam on a hairy string. Plus four smoking cigarette stubs, darting up and down in the gloom. I could make out their owners now. Nig, Nosy, Pam, and Pam's friend Mandy.

'No thanks,' I said as a square packet appeared under my nose. 'I don't smoke.'

'You what?' said Nig irritably. I could tell I'd made a bad start.

'I don't smoke,' I said again. 'Neither would you if you'd seen my friend Barry. He had clogged-up lungs. He used to cough so much at night I thought he was going to die. The doctor said cigarettes would kill him.'

Nig thought about that for a minute. When he spoke, his voice was dangerously low. 'You're not scared, are you? You're not a coward or something?'

'No,' I said. 'I just think smoking's daft.' This wasn't a brilliant move either. Everyone went stiff and quiet. I tried again. 'I'm not a coward and you know it. Or else why did you ask me to join your gang?'

Everyone relaxed. Mandy flicked her stub high in the

air and caught it between her teeth.

'Fair enough,' said Nig. 'Suit yourself then. But you've got to stick by the rest of the rules or you're out. Right?'

'Right,' I agreed. 'What rules?'

Pam and Nosy leaned forward. 'No telling anyone else what we do. No arguing with the leader. And no ducking out of a dare. We don't have chickens in the Garage Gang.'

'Fine,' I said between gulps. 'That sounds all right by me.' Then I waited for something to happen.

Nig sucked hard on his cigarette to keep it alight, crossing his eyes with the effort. Nosy tapped a long tube of ash onto the floor. Pam stuffed her fists into her pockets and stared at her feet. Mandy said nothing. She never did. She just sat there shuffling a handful of playing cards and spreading them out along her arm.

I began to fidget in my seat. If I had stayed at home, I could have watched the Saturday morning cartoons. I could have helped Gran with her latest jigsaw. I could have made a start on the model dinosaur Dad bought me at the museum last month.

I tugged at the knot in my scarf and managed to loosen it. Then I unwound it and let the ends hang down. I turned up my coat collar and twisted my mouth. I was hoping I looked like a private detective or a foreign spy.

'What's that?' hissed Nig, so suddenly my glasses slipped down my nose.

'What's what?' I whispered back. Why was everyone looking at me?

'You've brought someone with you, haven't you?' Nig was snarling now. 'I thought I told you to keep quiet about us.'

'But I did,' I protested as frantically as I could without raising my voice. 'I haven't got anyone to tell. Except for my sister Jackie, and she wouldn't want to know.'

Nig stood up slowly, like a grizzly bear tracking down its kill. He crept across to the garage doors and put his hand on the handle. The others sat up. This was more like it.

A moment later, a shaft of daylight stung our eyes and Nig shouted, 'Gotcha. You little creep.'

It was DD, the drippy kid from school. He hauled her inside, then pinned her against the door. She was only about half his size, but she didn't seem too bothered.

'What you want to tell her for?' Nig barked at me. 'I told you this was a secret, didn't I?'

'I didn't tell her,' I protested again. I could feel Pam breathing down my collar. 'It's not my fault. I don't know where she came from.'

'I followed him,' said DD in an amazingly chirpy voice. 'I follow Goggles everywhere. I saw him go down the alley, so I thought I'd go too.'

'Gawd,' said Nig in disgust. 'That's all we need.' He turned back to DD. 'Clear off, you little maggot,' he said. 'And if you ever tell anyone where we are, I'll...'

'Why can't she stay?' That was me. I could hardly believe it. The words just seemed to come out by themselves. But then, I'd never had a fan of my own before, and it seemed a shame to get rid of her straightaway. 'We weren't doing anything special, were we? So I can't see how it matters.' I'd done it now. There was a long, hostile pause.

After about a hundred years, Pam spoke. 'It's true, that,' she said. 'We haven't done anything interesting for months. Not since we found those shopping trolleys and had a chariot race round the car park.'

'Yeah,' said Nosy. 'It's true, that.' Mandy just nodded and shuffled her cards a bit faster.

Nig gave DD a shove in my direction. 'All right,' he said grudgingly. 'But she'd better not break any of the rules. That's all.'

'She won't,' I said with my fingers crossed. 'Will you, DD?'

DD beamed at me. She had even fewer teeth than Pam. 'Course not, Goggles. I'll do anything you say.' Then she looked around the garage as if it was the nicest place she'd ever visited. 'What a lovely little house,' she breathed. 'Can I tidy it up for you? I can stick some of my pictures on the walls. I'm a really good drawer.'

Nig swallowed a war cry. 'This is not a little house,' he began. 'This is a...'

But she wasn't listening. She was busily scraping up a pile of bent nails and trampled cigarette stubs using two pieces of mouldy cardboard. 'Do you meet every week?' she rattled on. 'Do you look for adventures and help the police capture bank robbers?'

'Gawd,' the Parker twins erupted together. Mandy sprayed her cards in the air and caught them in her pockets.

'No, we don't look for adventures.' Nig's voice was at its lowest and nastiest. 'We look for trouble. And if any banks want robbing, we're the ones to do it. Right?'

DD giggled. 'You are funny,' she said. 'What sort of trouble? Can we look for some now? Can we?'

Nig cracked his finger joints like a prize fighter limbering up. Then he made a sudden lunge at the door, which swung open with a rumble of rusting iron. 'You want trouble,' he said. 'You can have it. Come on.'

Mandy silently untied the torch from its string and packed it in her sports bag, while the rest of us stumbled out into the daylight, rubbing our eyes. DD skipped after Nig, and for one awful moment I thought she was going to hold his hand. But she didn't. She wheeled round and held mine.

Her palms felt horribly warm and sticky, as if she'd

been playing with school plasticine all morning. I pulled away and jammed my hands in my jacket pockets but she didn't seem to mind. 'Were you at a different school before you came to ours?' she asked happily. I was beginning to regret being kind to her, but her eyes were so shiny and admiring, I mumbled out some sort of reply.

'Yeah,' I said into my scarf. 'I had to leave home when I was little. They sent me to a special school, and I've only just been allowed out again.'

Nig stopped dead and spun round. Just for a second, the look on his face was a bit like DD's, all shiny and admiring. 'They sent you away?' he repeated. 'How old were you?'

'About six, I think,' I told him. 'Can't remember exactly. I was there for so long.'

Nig rattled his head and banged it with the side of his hand. He seemed to be shaking a loose screw into place. 'Six?' he kept saying. 'Six! My Dad says I'll end up in one of those places if I carry on the way I'm going. But I've never heard of anyone getting put away at six.' He was making me sound like a hero out of a comic.

'Look,' I tried to explain. 'It wasn't all that clever. It was only because...'

But he held up his hands to stop me, and backed away. I don't think his brain could take any more. Then he wandered off to catch up with the Parkers, still muttering 'Six!' to himself, and rattling his head.

'He's jealous,' announced DD proudly. 'He wants everyone to think he's the naughtiest boy in the school, but it looks as if you've beaten him to it.'

'Me?' I was puffing a bit, trying to keep up with her. 'I've never done anything much. I don't even eat sweets in class, in case I get caught.'

'Oh?' DD was skipping backwards now, and I could see she was puzzled. 'Why did they send you away to a special school then?'

Suddenly I understood. Nig had decided I was a real hooligan. He thought I'd been arrested when I was still at infants' school. Goodness knows what for. Biting the heads off teddy bears, or setting fire to the Wendy House, I suppose. I managed to grin, although my chest was nearly bursting and my legs had gone wobbly. 'Is that what you think?' I asked. 'Do you think I'm one of the baddies?'

'No,' said DD. 'I think you're just like Superman. You've even got the right glasses.' And if I hadn't sunk down quickly on a milk crate to give myself a rest, I've got a nasty feeling she would have tried to hug me.

'Oi!' came a cry from up ahead. 'This is it, gang. Now's your chance for a spot of business.' I staggered to my feet and went to see what was happening.

A series of twisting backways and alleys had brought us to a line of uneven fencing. Nig pushed against one of the wooden slats so that it swung upwards, and one by one we all crawled through the gap.

We were looking down on a railway track. If you don't live in London, you probably don't realize that the Underground isn't always under the ground at all. The further it gets away from the City and the famous tourist places, the closer it gets to the surface, until it starts popping up into the outside world.

Here, it just looked like any other sort of railway. A steep embankment on either side, overgrown with pink weeds and scattered with rubble. To our left was the mouth of a tunnel, dark and throbbing like a monster's lair. To our right the metal lines swooped past us and away into the distance, so that they seemed to touch before they disappeared.

'See those silver ones with the funny lumps,' said DD. 'They're electric, you know. They can frizzle you up in one second.'

'Mmm,' I said, sinking down again and leaning my back against a stack of concrete slabs. 'But they switch them off at night so the Fluffers can scrape them clean.' I hadn't walked so far in years. Well, come to think of it, I'd probably never walked so much in my entire life. Maybe I'd be able to think about running soon. But not yet.

'Right,' Nig was saying. 'We wait till we hear the train, then we run for it. Last one across the track is the champion, and anyone who bottles out is a chicken.'

'Yeah,' said Pam and Nosy, looking at me. 'And we don't have chickens in the Garage Gang, do we?' They scraped their heels against the rough grass and spat on their hands. Mandy dumped her bag on the ground and bent over like an Olympic sprinter.

I just stared at Nig. 'You're mad,' I said. 'You can get killed crossing the railway. Haven't you seen the warnings?'

Nig laughed in the back of his throat, as if he was gargling with salty water. 'Course we've seen the warnings. That's the whole point, isn't it? We've got to prove we're not scared. If it wasn't dangerous, we wouldn't bother, would we?'

'That's because you don't know what it's like, living in a wheelchair,' I shouted at him. I could hear a distant rumble and I was beginning to panic. 'There was a girl at my last school who broke her back, and she wouldn't have thought you were being brave or anything. She'd have thought you were round the bend.' I stood up stiffly. 'Come on, DD,' I said. 'I'm not letting you play stupid games.'

'Oi,' snapped Nig. 'You're breaking the rules.'

'Yeah,' said the twins. 'You have to do what the leader tells you. Remember?'

But I wasn't falling for that old trick. 'I don't have to do anything if I don't want to. Not if I think it's pathetic. And if this is what the Garage Gang calls fun, then you can count me out. I'd rather sit at home and watch the telly. At least I won't get my brains splattered all over the front of a driver's cab.'

The rumbling was even louder now, and as I started to heave myself up the bank, the train roared out of the tunnel. I turned to watch the carriages snake past us along the track. People stared out of the windows, frowning and pointing, and then they were gone, leaving me to face the gang. I knew I'd ruined their game but I was too tired to run away, so I stood with my back against the fence and waited for the trouble to start.

'He's right, you know,' said Pam slowly. 'Why don't we ever have any proper adventures, Nig? Why don't we ever do anything really exciting?'

'Yeah,' said Nosy. 'A proper adventure. Something really exciting.' Mandy nodded, then started juggling with three pebbles she'd found in the grass.

Nig gave his friends a look that would have turned anyone else to stone. 'Only adventure I want now is a bag of chips,' he snarled. 'With plenty of salt and vinegar. Come on you lot, or you can buy your own.' He stamped up the slope towards the loose fencing and as he pushed past me I could hear him muttering to himself again. 'Six! My Gawd. Six!'

Then the others scuttled after him, and DD and I were left alone.

3
Gran

'That's it then,' I said, as DD and I climbed back into the alley. 'We're out of the gang. Sorry.'

'No we aren't.' She sounded very sure of herself. I blinked at her from behind my glasses, so she giggled and went on, 'Nig would've punched you on the nose if he'd wanted to throw you out But he didn't, so that proves it. See?'

'Not really,' I began. 'I broke all the rules. I wouldn't smoke and I wouldn't play chicken, and anyone can see I don't fit in...'

'Doesn't matter.' We were in the main street now, and DD was skipping backwards again. All the shoppers were staring at her. 'Nig likes you because you're brave.'

'But I'm not.' I wished she wouldn't hop about like that. I was so embarrassed, my ears were starting to feel hot. 'I'm not brave at all.'

'Yes you are,' she insisted at the top of her voice. People turned to glare at both of us now. 'You're the bravest person in the world. Nig didn't want me in his gang, but you made him. And then you told him he was round the bend. No one's ever done that before, not even McAvity.'

'So Nig must hate me,' I argued. My face felt as if it was on fire. Thank goodness we were nearly home.

'No he doesn't. He likes you. And so do I.' DD

watched me climb up our front steps, then gave me a wave as Gran opened the door. 'Byeee,' she called, skipping along the pavement.

I didn't answer. I didn't want Gran to think I'd gone soft in the head.

'Is that your new little friend?' she asked, helping me out of my jacket and combing down my hair with her fingers.

'No,' I said fiercely. 'Just some daft kid. Can't seem to shake her off.' But I could tell from Gran's smile that she didn't believe me. She's too knowing by half, my Gran. She's always watching and listening and weighing things up. Sometimes she seems to know things about me before I even know them myself, which can be quite creepy at times. It's a bit like living with a mind reader, and I sometimes wonder if I've got any secrets at all.

For instance, Gran's brilliant at guessing when I'm in a bad mood and likely to pick a fight with Jackie. 'You've woken up with a devil on your shoulder this morning,' she says. 'See if you can sort out this jigsaw for me. I need all the bits of sky in one heap, and all the bits of grass in another.' And she keeps me so busy, I don't have time to start an argument with anyone.

Or else she'll open the door for me and say, 'You've done well at school today. You can have the little treat I've hidden in the fridge.' Or, 'Never mind, love. I've hired a nice new video to cheer you up.' And she's always right. I don't know how she does it.

She's even been known to tell the future, although she doesn't do that very often. Maybe it worries her. Anyway, she once told my Mum she was going to meet a tall, handsome stranger, and the very next day a man came round to mend our gas boiler. He looked just like an advert for coffee beans, and he was at least seven feet tall. How about that?

But the best time of all was when Gran told us we were

going on a long journey, and Jackie won a painting competition at the local arts centre. The prize was a family ticket for a film called 'Voyage To The Unknown Planet', and we could hardly watch it for laughing. I bet you're impressed now, aren't you? And I haven't even mentioned all her other predictions. Like the time she guessed the name of the royal baby before any of the papers knew, and the way she always knows who's going to win the World Cup.

Mind you, there are a few drawbacks too. The dreams, mainly. Or nightmares. Once or twice a year, Gran wakes up in the night shaking with fear and she won't tell us what she's seen. Sometimes she even sleep-walks, and in the morning we find her curled up under the kitchen table. I don't like that much. We think she's probably reliving the war and sheltering from the air raids, but Gran always refuses to talk about it so I don't really know.

Anyway, that Saturday she gave me a quick hug and said, 'Go on then.'

'Go on where?' I asked. Honestly, it's like one long 'knock-knock' joke in our house some days.

'Go and lie down in the other room. You're tired out. And that little kid isn't as daft as she looks, you know. You could trust her with your life.' Which was quite a strange thing to say about someone she'd only seen for two seconds, but I didn't have the energy to argue. I went and flopped in front of an old adventure film, and I was asleep before Gran came back with a pillow for my head.

After that, I think I must have dozed, on and off, for most of the weekend. Even Auntie Hat couldn't keep me awake when she came round for Sunday lunch, and that was pretty amazing because she's got a voice like a fog horn and she never, ever stops talking. She doesn't look a bit like Mum, and it's hard to believe they're really sisters at all, even when they're wearing their Fluffer dungarees. But they make each other laugh, so I suppose that's the main thing.

I didn't feel much like laughing, though. Monday morning came round far too fast, and I was back in the playground again before I knew it. Nig spotted me straight away. I wrapped my scarf round my face and tried impersonating the Invisible Man, but he wasn't fooled for one minute. He stamped across and I waited for the thumping to start.

'School,' he growled, kicking at the wall with his outsized boots and chipping chunks out of the brickwork. 'Why don't we bunk off for the week? Go and look for some decent trouble? You must know loads of places.'

So DD must have been right. Nig still liked me for some reason. All the same, I just couldn't fancy hiding in a smelly garage with him for days on end when I could be sitting in a nice warm classroom with proper radiators. I thought about it, but not for long. 'Not today,' I said. 'It's chocolate sponge for afters, and I want double helpings.'

Nig nodded. He could see the reasoning in that.

'You could have extras as well,' I told him. I was beginning to feel a bit mean about turning him down, and in any case I wanted to keep on the right side of his temper. He was never in the best of moods at school, mainly because McAvity was always moaning at him for something or other. So he spent half his time outside the Head Teacher's door, and I don't think he enjoyed a single lesson we had to do. He even hated swimming, although he never said so out loud.

'All you have to do is stay behind with me and help tidy up a few chairs,' I went on. 'It's brilliant. The cooks share out all the left-overs.'

Nig attempted to sneer, but I could see his mouth was

watering. I don't think his Mum ever gave him any breakfast, and he hardly ever had enough money for crisps. Perhaps that was why he used to spend his breaktimes twisting the First Years' arms.

'Don't like the sound of it,' he grumbled. 'Can't stand creeps.' The heavy boots were attacking the wall again. I swallowed hard.

'This has nothing to do with creeping. This is to do with second helpings.' The boots stopped just before they reached my shins.

So that was how Nig ended up stacking chairs in the dining hall with me most days. Nosy would stand outside with his face squashed against the window, mouthing rude comments, but we didn't care. We knew when we were on to a good thing.

'You got a dad?' asked Nig one lunch hour, as we mopped down the tables with soapy rags.

'No,' I said. 'Well, yes. But he doesn't live with us any more. I only see him once a month. It's dead boring. We walk round the dinosaur museum in the winter, and the zoo in the summer, and then we have a hamburger at the station.

'You're lucky.' Nig aimed his rag at the bucket, and sloshed foam over the floor tiles. 'Mine's at home. That's even worse. All he ever does is moan about the rent and watch the horse-racing on the goggle box.'

'Does he win?' I asked.

Nig made a disgusting noise by squishing his wet palms together. 'Fat chance. He's a born loser, my old man. That's what my Mum says, and she should know.'

DD was waiting for me when we went outside. I slipped her a small square of pudding, and she tagged along munching it while we wandered across the netball court to meet the Parkers and Mandy.

'I've been thinking,' said Pam.

'Wonders will never cease,' Nosy started, but she

kicked him and carried on.

'We ought to have a proper plan for the Garage Gang. Then we wouldn't have to sit around doing nothing every rotten week.'

'Ooh yes.' That was DD butting in, of course. No one else would have had the nerve. 'We could have a table tennis table. And a darts board. And a cupboard with orange squash in it. And bourbon biscuits.'

'Gawd.' Nosy stopped rubbing his sore leg. 'Sounds more like the Brownies. You'll have us all sitting on toadstools next.'

'Shuttup,' said Nig. 'Who's running this gang anyway? I'm the one who makes the plans around here, and don't you forget it.' Mandy shook her head, then nodded it. She wasn't taking any chances.

'OK,' said Pam. 'So what're we doing this week?'

'Wait and see,' Nig told her. No one really believed he had any ideas, but even DD had enough sense not to say so.

'Right,' bellowed McAvity that afternoon, when everyone had more or less stopped talking. 'New topic.'

People sat up and looked interested.

'History...'

People sagged back and groaned.

'... of transport,' McAvity battled on regardless. 'Could involve art, science, geography, all sorts. Plenty of detective work. Libraries. Museums. All that kind of business...'

This was the way McAvity usually talked, in short bursts like sniper-fire to keep us from interrupting. We never knew when he was going to run out of ammunition or cease fire altogether.

'... tape recorders. Interview drivers. Draw a few graphs. Bit of computer nonsense. Impress the governors. Understand me?'

We all nodded energetically. Mandy's head nearly fell off. This was the only way to stop him talking and get any work done at all.

'Right then.' He reloaded and let loose one last round of bullets. 'Take home private worksheets. Fill in what you can. Collect pictures, old photographs, bus tickets. Start scrap books. Decorate folders. Pamela Parker, stop yawning. Give out craft paper.' He leaned against the blackboard to recover while Pam sorted out the rest of us.

'Blue paper for the girls, red paper for the boys. That way, Sir's going to know which folders are which when he marks them.' Pam believed in women's rights, and the blue paper was about twice as shiny as the red. My piece was all faded round the edges, and someone had once stood a cup of coffee on it because I could still see the brown stain.

I did what I could with it, folding it in half and writing my name in large capitals across the front. Then I drew a railway track in and out of the letters, turning the final 'R' into a tunnel. I was just copying a picture of a tube train out of a class library book, when the door opened and DD trotted in with a note for McAvity. She winked and grinned at me while he looked at it, and did her best to see my drawing although I covered it with my arms.

McAvity coughed and banged his chest, so that a faint cloud of dust flew out of his jumper. 'A reminder. Hope no one here needs it. From London Transport. Children seen fooling about near busy lines. Playing on embankments. Very dangerous. Lethal. Also out-of-bounds. Against law. Offenders could be prosecuted.'

'Please, sir,' said DD grinning like a letter box. 'Does that mean you could get your head chopped off?'

'Nah,' called out Nosy. 'That's executed. If you're persecuted, you get thrown to the lions, don't you sir?'

32

McAvity leaned against the blackboard again and snapped a stick of chalk in two. Then he rattled out, 'Not persecuted, Parker. Prosecuted. Means you get fined. Hundreds of pounds. Quite right too. Understand?'

We all nodded, more frantically than ever. Mandy hit her nose on her desk and DD scooted off to the next class, waving at me round the crack in the door before she closed it.

After tea that evening, I unrolled my worksheet on the living room table and started to tick off as many boxes as I could. '1. Talk to as many drivers as you can - car, taxi, lorry, bus, train, etc. Find out what they like or dislike about driving. 2. Investigate transport of the past. Talk to an old person, read books, or look at pictures. 3. Try to visit one of the following - a railway station, a bus depot, a taxi firm, a museum.'

Well, the first question was pretty hopeless. No one in our family was a driver because we didn't have a car. Mum couldn't afford one; Gran preferred the buses, and Dad had been disqualified for knocking down a wall outside the police station.

'He's still a driver,' said Gran. 'You could ask him what it feels like to be off the road.' She shook her head and made sucking noises through her teeth. 'I hate cars. They're nothing but trouble. Traffic jams and exhaust fumes and noise. If it was up to me, they'd all be banned, but no one ever listens to people like me these days.'

'I will,' I said. 'You can help me with the second question. Tell me what it was like in the old days.'

'Not so much of the old, thank you very much.' She pretended to cuff me round the ear, but I ducked out of the way and found a stump of pencil down the side of my chair.

'Go on,' I said. 'You used to be a Fluffer once, didn't

you? Tell me what it was like down the tube stations in the war. There were some pictures in a book at school today, and I saw loads of people sleeping on the escalators in blankets. Only the stairs weren't moving, of course.' I giggled and got ready to write, but Gran had suddenly gone quiet. Usually she talks all the time, like a clockwork parrot.

I looked up and saw a strange, blank expression on her face. She wasn't frowning and she wasn't smiling. It was almost as though she'd put on a plastic mask to hide her real self.

'You were down there in the war, weren't you?' I pestered. 'You must remember it all, Gran. Was it exciting? Were you scared? Did the stations ever get bombed?'

I waited, but she still didn't answer. It's a very odd thing, but until that moment it hadn't ever struck me how much Gran hated our local tube station. She never went near the place if she could help it. She either caught a bus or she walked, unless she was going somewhere special and then she phoned for a taxi. And now I came to think about it, she didn't talk about the war much either. I decided to change the subject.

'What about the buses, then? Were they the same as ours? Did they have automatic doors and ticket machines? Did the drivers wear uniforms?'

Something seemed to click inside Gran's brain, and she was back to normal again, chattering away about clippies and trams and women engineers.

'We all had to help, you see. There weren't enough men to go round any more. And a very good job we made of it too. I was on the old City route myself for quite a while, and I'd still be there if the soldiers hadn't come home and pinched all the best jobs off us. Shall I tell you about the skid test? Now there's an experience to make your hair stand on end. You can forget about

34

all your expensive fairgrounds and roller coasters. There's nothing to beat a double decker bus on a sheet of oily water.'

This was more like it. By the time Gran had finished, I had a whole page of notes for McAvity, plus a creased brown photograph of a girl in a buttoned jacket.

'That's my Gran,' I told the class next morning. 'She used to work on the buses in the war, and she says she still misses it. Once, a man left his teeth on the back seat and someone else went and sat on them. And another time, a doctor left a skeleton in the luggage rack, but I don't know if that's really true.'

So far, this new topic wasn't turning out to be half as boring as I'd expected, and on Saturday, Dad was supposed to be coming over for his monthly visit. Perhaps I could persuade him to take me to the Transport Museum or somewhere like that. At least it would make a change from dinosaurs and stuffed birds.

Some hopes.

'Sorry, love,' said Mum when she opened the post on Thursday morning. 'Your Dad's written to say he's in bed with a nasty flu' bug so he can't make it this week. You'll have to see him next Saturday instead.'

Normally I wouldn't have minded too much. I was sick of the same old routine, and I wasn't particularly desperate for a station hamburger. But just for once I'd been looking forward to my outing with Dad. This was partly because of McAvity's topic, but more because I wanted a good excuse to get out of the Garage Gang.

Somehow I just couldn't stand the thought of another Saturday morning in that smoke-filled dump, and I didn't have much faith in Nig's secret plans either. I had a horrible feeling they were going to involve some sort of bother with the law. Smashing windows, or breaking into the games hut at school, or swiping videos from the corner shop. Those were the sort of things Nig found exciting, and I suppose he was right in a way, if you liked being chased down subways by angry policemen. But it wasn't my idea of fun. Apart from anything else, I wouldn't have known how to face Mum and Gran if I got caught.

So I knew exactly what would happen. Nig would stand up in the garage and say, 'OK. Let's go and look for trouble,' and I would say, 'No. Sorry. I'm going home.' And this time, Nig would blow my cover. He'd finally realize that I wasn't the world's greatest villain after all. I was just a feeble, drippy coward who'd never done a brave thing in my entire life. The thought of what he was likely to do to me made my bottom lip tremble, and I rubbed at my scar. What a rotten mess. What was I going to do?

'Cheer up,' said Mum, who must have been thinking I was still upset about Dad. 'I'll tell you what. I'll have a word with Sergeant Major Figgs in the ticket office tonight. If I can butter him up with a nice cup of hot chocolate, I'm sure he'll let you have a look round the station at the weekend. How about that?'

I brightened up. Figgsy wasn't a proper sergeant major at all. The Fluffers just called him that because he tried to boss everyone about, but really he was quite a good sort.

'Brilliant,' I said. 'Would he let me bring some of my friends too?'

Mum widened her eyes. 'Friends? How many?' I hadn't got round to telling her much about the Garage Gang yet. I'd been putting it off.

'Um,' I said, counting on my fingers. 'Nig, Nosy, Pam. They're the main ones. Then there's Mandy, but she's practically invisible. And DD. I suppose I'll have to ask her as well, because she'll tag along anyway.'

Mum's eyebrows disappeared under her fringe, and

she toasted herself another slice of bread to keep her strength up. 'Well! Six of you. I don't know. Poor old Figgsy isn't keen on kids. Says they upset his stomach, but I'll do my best for you.'

I gave her a quick hug. She smelt of dust and disinfectant and strong soap. Then I grabbed my swimming things and hurried off to school.

'Got any plans for Saturday yet?' I asked Nig at lunchtime.

'Yeah. One or two.' He seemed a bit cagey, which shouldn't have surprised me.

'Oh, magic,' I said, hoping I sounded enthusiastic enough for him. 'I can hardly wait.' Then I dumped down a heap of chairs and added, just in passing, as if it didn't matter in the slightest, 'My Mum says she might be able to fix it for us to go down the Tube. For a sort of guided tour. See how everything works. She can't promise of course, but...'

'Yeah. All right then.'

I hadn't expected Nig to take the bait so easily. Maybe he'd been really stuck for ideas. Or maybe he liked the thought of blaming someone else if the whole adventure was a flop. Anyhow, the next minute we had to rush off to catch the swimming coach and bag the back row for the rest of the gang, so that was the end of the discussion. Pam and Nosy would probably go along with anything, so long as it made a change, and Mandy wasn't likely to argue. So that was all right.

I made the most of the afternoon. I didn't know how much longer my fame was going to last, so I was determined to enjoy it while I could. In the changing room, I peeled off my shirt very slowly, then I spent ages unrolling my towel and hanging my stuff on a peg. I knew everyone wanted a look at my chest, so I thought I might as well give them a decent show.

The lesson went well too. Our group was getting

ready for the end-of-term swimming gala, so I was practising tag racing with Pam and Nosy. I liked the bit where we had to spin underwater to turn round, and I almost managed to beat Mandy when we played 'Treasure Hunt'. The teacher threw in dozens of heavy rubber rings, and we had to collect as many as we could from the bottom of the pool before she blew her whistle. I had never held my breath for so long before, and I took much longer than usual to feel tired.

All the same, I was glad to sit down afterwards and rub myself dry while Nig told me some more of his weird jokes. He was in a good mood because he'd been let off swimming that day. His Mum had written a note to the school saying he had a wart on his foot but no one had ever seen him limping. It's a wonder McAvity hadn't demanded some proof, but maybe he wasn't too keen on inspecting Nig's feet.

Back in the coach, I made sure I sat next to Mandy. She was something solid to lean on, and I was pretty sure she wouldn't complain. Also, she had that sort of short, springy hair that didn't drip over other people.

'You look pleased with yourself,' said Gran when I staggered up our front steps. 'I expect you'll be glad of a sandwich.' It was already made. A great, fat tower of bread wrapped round a chopped banana. See what I mean about my Gran?

I was halfway through this feast when Jackie flung herself into the hall and flopped down on a chair. Art folder, jacket, woolly hat and books spread themselves round her feet on the kitchen floor. My sister was always fond of making a dramatic entrance. Some people say it's because of her artistic temperament, whatever that might be, but I reckon it's just because she likes to show off.

'This is it,' she was saying dreamily. 'This could be my big chance. My name in lights. My designs in all the fashion magazines. My very own label. Paris, here I come.'

The whole point of this was to make Gran and me say, 'Ooooh! What? Tell us all about it. Please.' But my mouth was full of squashed banana, and Gran could see straight through that sort of trick, so in the end Jackie had to give in and explain without waiting for us to prompt her.

'It's a competition, run by all the best fashion designers in the country. They're looking for the ten most promising young artists to put on a show in a big hotel at the end of the year.' She whipped a small press cutting out of her pencil case and plonked it on the table.

'Design an Original Collection,' it said. 'Fun-Wear for Work and Play, Day and Night, Evening and Leisure.' Underneath was a long list of rules, plus a description of the prizes in flashy lettering. No wonder Jackie was starry-eyed. If she could be one of the winners she wouldn't have to be a Fluffer, and she'd never have to wear dungarees to work. Not ever.

Gran read the instructions over my shoulder. 'Not long till the closing date,' she pointed out. 'You'll have to get a move on.'

'I know.' Jackie sat forward and stuck her chin in her hands. 'One week to produce a whole range of clothes. Six outfits all based on one theme.'

'Six dresses?' I wiped my glasses and gaped at her. It had once taken her three weeks to sew round a glove puppet.

'No, stupid.' Jackie certainly knew how to make me feel important. 'Just the art work. But that's bad enough. I haven't even got a springboard yet.' My face must have crinkled up at that, because she went on, 'You know. A main title. Something like, "On Safari", or "Roaring Twenties", or "Space City".'

'So what's wrong with those?' I asked. 'They sound OK to me.' Stork-women would probably look almost acceptable in astronaut suits and goldfish bowl helmets.

'It's all been done before,' Jackie complained. 'I've got to think of something totally new. Totally different.'

'You've got to guess the shape of the future,' said Gran thoughtfully. 'The colour everyone's going to want in a year's time. The right sort of material. The right sort of patterns. The whole look.'

Jackie did the gaping this time. 'Where did you learn all that, Gran?' she burbled.

Gran laughed. 'Where d'you think? I haven't spent my life in a paper bag, you know. I have seen a bit of the world.' She wandered over to fill the kettle. 'Green and brown,' she said firmly, as the water gushed out of the tap. 'Natural materials like cotton and wool and silk. And stick to a style that's simple but comfortable. You'll knock the judges for six.'

Jackie laughed. You couldn't blame her. Gran spent her life wearing second-hand cardigans and droopy skirts. She was hardly a famous name in the world of fashion.

But for all that, I had a funny feeling she knew exactly what she was talking about. And I couldn't help remembering the creased brown photograph in my topic folder. It was strange to think that the pretty, smiling girl was still hiding inside my Gran somewhere, almost as though the grey hair and wrinkles were nothing but a clever disguise.

4
Jack the Lad

Mum popped into my room to say goodnight before she rushed off to work, and the creaking of the door woke me up.

'You won't forget to ask about me and the gang, will you?' I reminded her, mumbling the words into my pillow. I was dead beat after all the swimming and diving.

'Of course not,' she said. 'But don't set your heart on anything. You know what the Sergeant Major's like. We'll have to keep our fingers crossed and hope he's in a cheerful mood tonight.'

He must have been. Or else the hot chocolate soothed his dodgy stomach, because next morning at breakfast Mum gave me the go-ahead. 'Eleven o'clock at the ticket office on Saturday morning. I'll be there to give old Figgsy the nod. But for goodness sake tell your friends not to muck around or give him any bother, or I'll never hear the end of it.'

'OK,' I said, although my insides weren't so sure. I'd never seen Nig on his best behaviour, and I didn't think he could be polite if he tried. His idea of good manners was to take off his jacket before he hit you. Still, I passed on the news when I got to school and he seemed pleased enough.

The next day I trailed off to meet the gang with my scarf flapping dismally in the breeze. I knew Gran would be watching me through the front window, and I hoped she couldn't read my mind from a distance.

This is a big mistake, I kept thinking. I just know I'm going to end up regretting it.

DD was waiting for me by the alley, and when we reached the garage it was already thick with smoke.

'Come on then,' said Pam as soon as we joined the circle. 'What's Wonder Boy got planned for us today?'

'Yeah,' said Nosy. 'Nig says we've all got to take it in turns to look for trouble. And you're the first.'

Four cigarette stubs glinted at me, and my tongue stuck to the roof of my mouth like a strip of velcro.

'Go on, Goggles,' said DD, hopping about as if she hadn't a care in the world. I suppose she hadn't.

'Well. We're going down the Underground,' I croaked. 'Sort of private guided tour. My Mum's arranged it with her boss.'

Everyone seemed to stop breathing. The red lights wobbled in the air like confused glow worms.

'Hang about,' said Nosy. 'It's "No Smoking" down there, isn't it?'

'Doesn't matter.' Pam threw her stub on the floor and crushed it under her foot. 'We've run out of ciggies anyway.'

'Yeah. Stop griping,' said Nig. 'You said you wanted something to do, so let's go and do it.' He stood up, and they all made a move towards the door. 'Follow me,' he growled over his shoulder. 'Keep quiet and keep your eyes open. This little game could be very useful if we all remember what we're supposed to be looking for.'

'Yeah.' Nosy and Pam were right behind him. 'Trouble.'

Mandy gave me a slow, meaningful nod. I nodded back without any meaning at all, while she unhitched the torch and packed it in her bag. Then we all

42

muscled our way outside like a party of gangsters off to a show-down, and Nosy kicked the door shut behind us with an echoing clang.

The others hardly spoke, but DD hung on to my elbow and chattered all the way to the station entrance. I could see Mum, dressed in a pink tracksuit, leaning against the ticket booth.

'Here they are,' she was telling Figgsy through the glass hatch. 'They're everso grateful to you for all your trouble, Mr Figgs.' She shoved me forwards and beamed at the rest of the gang. I suppose she thought they must be really sweet, nicely behaved children if they were bothering to make friends with a drip like me. 'Don't be late,' she called as she turned to go. 'I'm cooking supper for half past twelve.'

'Supper?' repeated DD, standing on one leg with curiosity.

'Mmm,' I said. 'That's what Mum calls it. She goes to bed in the afternoon.'

Figgsy coughed loudly and tapped on the glass. 'Round the side,' he was mouthing. 'Through the office door. Mind the saucer.'

We trooped past some posters advertising Kew Gardens and cheap rail tickets, until we came to a sign marked 'Staff Only', fixed on the peeling paintwork.

'Is it the toilets?' whispered DD.

'Nah,' answered Nig. 'Head Office. Obvious.' He shoved with his shoulder and the door swung inwards.

It reminded me of those pictures that photographers use at the seaside. You know. At the front there's a painting of a jolly, fat family in swimsuits, and people pay to put their heads through the holes where the faces should be, so it looks as though they're all having a great time in the sun. But really they're still wearing their raincoats and wellingtons.

Figgsy's office was a bit like that. Outside, when you

bought your tickets, all you could see was a stern face frowning at you through the window. Inside was a shabby, untidy room with a pile of dirty mugs in the sink. On the floor was a saucer of mashed sardines, and perched on a high stool was the back view of Mr Figgs. His shirt was sticking out from under his jacket, and I couldn't help noticing he was wearing a pair of tartan slippers.

'One minute,' he said, dealing a handful of small change into the shute and firing a stream of tickets at a group of tourists. 'Now then.' He twisted round and eyed us with suspicion. I didn't blame him. The way Nig was studying the cash dispenser would have made anyone a bit jumpy. 'So. You've come to find out how we run a tube station, have you? Something to do with your school project, or so I'm told. Is that right?'

'Yes, Sergeant. I mean, Mr Figgs,' I assured him. I hoped Mandy was making a good job of her nodding act, but I didn't dare look round in case he thought I was acting the fool. 'And we'd be really grateful for anything you can tell us. Or show us.'

'Yeah. Like chocolate machines and how to fiddle them,' Nig muttered down my ear.

I don't think Figgsy heard, because he treated us to a stiff smile. 'Well,' he said. 'To be honest, there's not a lot to see. We're due to have the whole place redecorated next week, so we're in rather a mess at the moment. And as you probably know, our lifts have been out of order for the last couple of days. But I can get one of the lads to show you round the platforms, and then you can ask him any questions about the signals and so on. Will that do for you?'

I doubted whether the Garage Gang would be particularly thrilled, but I thanked him again and he shouted some foreign-sounding words into an intercom machine. I think he was asking for one of his men to come to the office, but the message came out as, 'Missermiff. Kumastares. Ryoway.'

An enormous cat slithered down from Figgsy's lap and began to attack the sardines as if they were still alive. It dragged the largest chunk underneath the stool and growled over it happily.

Figgsy tried again. 'Harro? Missermiff. Noffiss pliss. Ryoway. Kyew.'

This time, the door flew open. 'All right, all right,' grumbled the Lad. He looked about ninety-six to me. He was so old, he made Figgsy look young. 'This the school party is it? Follow me then. Look sharp.'

He shot back outside again, and stamped away down a covered passage while the Garage Gang frantically tried to keep up. Every two seconds he would shout, 'This way!' and disappear down some steps or round a corner. I had never noticed before quite how many entrances and exits there were. I suppose I'd always been with Mum or Dad, so I'd only ever taken one line into town or back again. Now, the station was beginning to feel more like the maze at Hampton Court, except it was an awful lot scruffier.

Pieces of scaffolding were lying in the corridors, or propped together in small towers, and someone had already started chipping loose tiles off the walls. There was litter too, most of it scattered around the bins.

'Bloomin' public,' grumbled the Lad, half to himself and half to us. 'Can't aim properly. Always chuck stuff on the ground. Guess who has to clear it all up. Makes me sick.' He talked just like someone else I knew. McAvity. That was it.

'Have you worked here very long?' I asked, hoping to get him off the subject of rubbish and on to something more interesting.

'Long?' he exploded. 'Long? I should say so. Before you lot was born. Before your Mums was born, I shouldn't wonder.' He stopped and patted the tiled wall fondly. 'Been here all my working life. Man and boy. Should have retired, but they can't get rid of me. Stayed on part time. This way.'

With that he scooted off again. I could hear the others behind me, cracking jokes about him and imitating his creaky voice. 'Makes me sick. Man and boy. This way. This way.' Nig was copying the man's walk, dragging his leg in a lop-sided limp which everyone found hilarious.

'He's very old, isn't he?' said DD, who had stuck to me like a shadow all the way.

'Must be,' I said. 'About the same age as my Gran, I should think.'

To our left I spotted a 'Keep Out' sign next to a bricked-up archway, and I was so busy dodging round smashed tiles that I nearly tripped over our ancient guide. He had stopped to adjust his socks, and his dusty blue hat clung to his head as if it had been stuck on with super glue. I wondered if he ever took it off. He seemed so proud of it I could imagine him wearing it in bed.

'Where does that go?' I asked, pointing at the brickwork the builders had uncovered. I was glad of a chance to stop and get my breath back. In spite of his limp, the old man couldn't half move.

'Nowhere,' he said with a chuckle. 'Been bricked up, hasn't it?' He was obviously pleased with his answer because he smiled for the first time, and the tiny white bristles on his chin made an upside-down halo.

'But it must have gone somewhere once,' DD chimed in. 'Why did they block it off like that? Was there an accident or something?'

The smile drooped and the bristles stopped twinkling. 'It was just an extra passageway,' snapped the Lad. 'Wasn't really needed. Got rid of it years ago, before the end of the war. This way.'

46

DD looked at me and we both shrugged. We knew he wasn't telling us the whole story, but there wasn't much we could do about it.

We turned a final corner, and found ourselves on one of my usual platforms. I recognized the plastic seats and the faded posters that curved up the walls.

'See that map,' the Lad was saying. He was beginning to sound croaky now, like McAvity at the end of a noisy lesson.

We all crowded forward to look at a wallchart of the Underground system. Blue lines and red lines, criss-crossed neatly with brown and green, yellow and black. One junction had been rubbed almost bare by thousands of grubby fingers, but I could just make out the name of our own station.

'Seen that before,' said Nig in a bored voice. 'About a billion times.'

'So you might have,' said the Lad. 'But I bet you didn't know it was all wrong, did you?'

We frowned at him. How could it possibly be wrong? It was printed everywhere. Diaries, leaflets, address books. And I'd used it myself, loads of times whenever Dad took me out for the day. It had always got us to where we wanted to go.

'What's up with it then?' demanded Nosy, looking up from the litter bin he'd been exploring. 'Did the printers rip you off or something?'

The Lad grinned. His teeth were perfectly white and straight, and his gums were incredibly pink. Anyone could see that this was his favourite part of the tour. The 'not-many-people-know-this' part. 'It's only an artist's impression, not a real map at all. Invented by a man called Harry Whatsisname, and all very clever I'm sure.'

He took a deep breath, coughed, and let us wait for a minute. Then he went on. 'Of course, if you want to

47

get from here to Wimbledon, say, it'll do the job for you. But your actual tunnels are nothing like that.'

'You mean, they aren't all painted in pretty colours,' said Nig, smirking round at the Parkers and Mandy. He liked to make grown ups look stupid.

'I mean, they aren't neat and tidy like ruler lines. They aren't straight. They twist and they turn. They wriggle all over the place. They pop out of the ground and they dive back down again. There's even a network of secret tunnels deep below all the rest, and they're not shown at all.'

He prodded the map with a long, yellow fingernail. 'If you tried to draw the system properly, it'd look like a barrow load of snakes. No one would ever find where they were to start with, let alone where they were going.'

I stared hard at the poster. Behind it, I was sure I could see a curved ridge in the tiling which ran high above the map to form an archway. The other end of the bricked-up passageway. It must have been a useful short cut at one time. Why on earth had anyone wanted to hide it?

The Lad pulled up his sleeve to look at his watch. His cuff had frayed, and his wrist was covered in knobbly blue veins. 'Time for my tea break,' he announced. 'No wonder I was getting dry. This way.'

He lurched off again to the end of the platform, gave us a hurried description of the way the signals worked, then nipped through an opening marked 'No Entry'.

We found ourselves chasing him up a steep stairwell that made my head spin. After about thirty steps and four turns I had to rest. My heart seemed to be hammering against my stitches like a prisoner trying to escape from a locked dungeon.

'You go on,' I gasped to the others. 'I'll catch you up.'
'Thought you were the one who didn't smoke,'

sneered Nosy. 'You sound worse than my Grandad when he gets up in the morning.'

Nig was wheezing a bit, so he didn't waste his breath insulting me. He didn't need to. I could imagine what he was thinking. And as Pam and Mandy elbowed past, they made sure I came in for plenty of accidental digs in the ribs. I had an uncomfortable feeling that the visit hadn't been a stunning success.

'Well, I've had a brilliant time.' That was DD, of course, sitting three steps above me and hugging her knees. 'I like going down tunnels. It's sort of scary, isn't it? Like hunting for dragons or invading magic castles.'

'If you say so,' I gasped. 'I think I'm OK now. Let's get this over with.' I hauled myself up the last couple of flights, and was relieved to discover we were back in the corridor with the peeling door. I knocked softly and we went in.

The Lad was washing up a collection of chipped mugs under a cold water tap, and Mandy was scraping spoonfuls of lumpy coffee out of a jar. A kettle was rattling to itself underneath Figgsy's seat.

'Any questions before you go?' The voice came from the side of Figgsy's mouth, and I wondered why he hadn't been given a proper swivel chair. He catapulted two tickets through the hatch, then squirmed round to inspect us again. He pretended to like what he saw, but I could tell he wasn't exactly overjoyed.

'Yeah.' Pam folded her arms and gave him one of her squinty looks. 'I've got a question. Do you have women drivers on the Tube?' If poor old Figgsy dared to say the women weren't strong enough, he was going to be awfully sorry.

'Bloomin' women,' said the Lad, sloshing boiling water into the mugs and passing them round. 'They're everywhere these days. Can't keep them out.'

I helped myself to a dollop of milk out of a bottle. It

smelt slightly strange. 'Women used to work for London Transport in the war,' I said. 'I don't think they were allowed to drive, but they did everything else. Lots of them were engineers, and my Gran was on the buses. She really liked it.'

Pam grunted. I think that meant she was satisfied. She filled her mouth with coffee, then swallowed it very, very slowly. Figgsy looked hopefully round at the rest of us, waiting for some sign of interest.

Mandy sat on the floor juggling with three stale biscuits to amuse the cat. Nosy shovelled several heaps of wet sugar into his mug and stirred the mixture for about five minutes. When he had finished he left the spoon sticking up, and every time he took a gulp I thought he was going to poke out his eye. Nig stared at the blobs of cream floating on the top of his drink and moved his lips rhythmically. He was either practising his thank you speech, or going through every swear word he knew.

I desperately wanted to please Figgsy, but my head was empty. I couldn't think of a single thing to ask. Unless...

'We went past a tunnel that had been all cemented up,' said DD. 'Is there a story about it? Is it haunted? Is it full of vampire bats and spiders like a ghost train?'

'Well,' began Figgsy, almost spilling his coffee in surprise. 'It's funny you should say that, because during the war there was a late service for the work parties, and everyone called that the Ghost Train. I'm told it used to wake people up when they were sheltering from the air raids, but that was all a bit before my time. As for a hidden walkway, I'm afraid that's a mystery to me. You'll have to ask one of my lads. Do you know anything about it, Jack?'

The Lad looked as though he'd just been hit round the head with a bag of bricks. 'You finished with them

50

mugs?' he demanded, stepping between his boss and DD. 'I haven't got time to sit here gossiping all day. I haven't cleared the litter off the embankment yet.'

I looked at the office clock. It was nearly a quarter past twelve. 'I've got to go,' I said, jumping up and handing my mug to Jack the Lad. 'Thanks everso much for showing us round. It's been really useful. Especially all that stuff about the map and the signals.'

The others made various muffled comments, which luckily no one understood, and DD gave the station cat a farewell hug. Then we all backed out through the doorway and walked silently round to the front of the ticket office, where Figgsy was nodding at us behind the glass. We waved at him, piled down the steps and charged along the pavement until we were sure we were out of hearing range.

'Lousy waste of rotten time,' snarled Nosy. 'Who wants to do topic work on a rotten lousy Saturday morning?'

'I thought it was funny,' said DD. 'That old man had false teeth you know.'

'Suppose the tooth fairy mugged him in the night,' said Pam. 'Serves him right. Silly old fool.'

Mandy folded up a leaflet about fare dodgers, flicked it with her wrist and made it disappear.

I waited anxiously for Nig to speak. If he was mad at me, I'd be thrown out of the Garage Gang, which I didn't mind. But on the other hand, school would go back to being lonely and miserable, which I didn't fancy either. I could see I was in what Nig's Dad would have called a no-win situation.

'I reckon.' Nig spoke so slowly that I wanted to scream. Each word was like Chinese water torture. 'It was about as interesting as watching a slug race. But it wasn't a complete waste of time.'

He made a signal with his hands and we all put our

heads together in a sort of rugby scrum. DD couldn't quite reach, so she bounced up and down on the outside and tried to climb up my jacket.

'Let's just say...' Nig was being the big chief again, all mysterious and superior, '...I noticed one or two little details some of you probably missed. Little opportunities, shall we say. Especially for anyone who's serious about looking for trouble.' He tapped the side of his nose at us, and we all nodded. I don't think any of us knew why.

'What did he mean?' asked DD as she dragged me home. 'What little details? Opportunities for what?'

'You heard him,' I said darkly. 'Trouble.'

What had I started now? I hadn't planned all this so that the Garage Gang could give Figgsy an upset stomach. I didn't want anyone to mess up the station for Jack the Lad. The whole idea of the visit had been to avoid trouble, not cause it. But then, it just wasn't my day.

Half way through our midday meal, I started to tell the family all about the things we had seen and the awful coffee we'd had to drink. I had just got to the bit about the concealed passage, when Gran suddenly pushed back her chair and walked out of the room. It was her favourite pudding, too. Bananas and custard.

'Don't worry about it,' said Mum. 'She's a bit touchy about that tube station. That's all.'

'But why?' I asked. 'I thought she used to be a Fluffer. She's not afraid of the trains, is she?'

Mum shook her head and shared out Gran's banana between Jackie and me.

'Your Gran's a very brave woman,' she said. 'I've never heard all the details, because it all happened before I was born, but I know she used to do voluntary work for the Red Cross in the war. She helped rescue people during the Blitz, and went into ruined buildings

52

while the bombs were still falling. Your Auntie Hat reckons she saved quite a few lives. But...'

She spooned up a slice of banana and chewed it carefully. '...talking about the Underground upsets her. It's all to do with the war, of course, and she's explained most of it to your Auntie Hat and me. But it's Gran's story and I've promised to keep it a secret.'

She paused, swallowed some custard and gave me a smile. 'Don't worry. I'm sure she'll tell you all about it one day. In her own good time.'

Another pause, another mouthful of banana. 'Still, you can imagine what she said when Hat told her we were both going to be Fluffers. She nearly had a fit.'

'So why did you?' I asked, putting down my spoon. 'If you knew she was going to hit the roof.'

Mum grinned. 'Ask your sister,' she said. 'She'll understand.'

Jackie looked up from the picture she was drawing. 'Yep,' she said. 'When you're young, you never want to do what you're asked to do. You always want to do the opposite. It's like a sort of challenge, and you can't resist.' She took out a silver felt pen and went back to her stork-women.

'That's it,' agreed Mum. 'I must say I felt a bit guilty at first, but the station's so handy...' She scraped up the last of her custard and prodded at the pattern in the bottom of her bowl. 'Anyway, it's best not to ask her about it. If you want to find out about the history of the Tube, why don't you ask Mr Figgs?'

'We tried that,' I said. 'But I don't think he knows any more than you do. And the other man...'

'Jack Smith? White hair, false teeth, hates litter? Should have retired about ten years ago?'

'That's him. He kept changing the subject. We only wanted to ask him about the hidden tunnel. The workmen uncovered it when they knocked the old tiles off the wall.'

'I know the one you mean,' said Mum. 'Bricked up, isn't it? Well, it seems there was a direct hit one night during the raids, and there was such a lot of damage to that passage, they didn't bother to repair it. Too expensive, I suppose. So they just sealed it off. Makes sense, really.'

'Is that all?' I was disappointed. Why had Jack the Lad been so secretive about a collapsed ceiling?

Mum began to stack the dishes. 'It's all anyone round here will ever tell you I'm afraid. This area was more like a village in the old days. Everyone knew everybody else. And this happens to be one thing they still prefer to keep to themselves.'

She threw me a tea towel. Jackie was miles away, nibbling bits of banana in between scribbling on a notepad, so I was in charge of drying up.

'I shouldn't let it bother you,' said Mum as she filled the bowl with foamy water. 'You must have a lovely lot of material for your transport folder now. It'll be nice to get a good report from your new teacher, won't it?'

'Mmmm,' I said, wiping my cloth round a dirty plate. McAvity wasn't the main person on my mind at that moment. My head was full of the Garage Gang. Figgsy. Jack the Lad.

And Gran.

5
Stork-women

DD was in the habit of walking to school with me by this time. Every morning she would be waiting at the corner of the street, and it didn't matter how fast I tried to shift, she was always skipping along backwards beside me, grinning as if she'd won me in a raffle. She didn't seem to realize how embarrassing this was.

I could see the looks on the Parkers' faces whenever the pair of us arrived at the school gates together, and it didn't take much imagination to guess what sort of comments they were making about me under their breath. Nosy still hadn't forgiven me for wasting his Saturday morning, and I don't think Pam wanted to keep me in the gang for many more weeks either. So it was useful to have DD to blame.

'Why can't you find someone your own age to pester?' I snapped at her one morning, when I saw Mandy studying us from the top rung of the climbing frame. DD's eyes went all watery, but I didn't care. I'd had enough. 'Look,' I almost shouted. 'Can't you see you're making me feel a fool? Everyone's laughing at me. They think you're my girl friend.'

'Well, I'm not,' she shouted back. 'I'm your friend, and I'm a girl. That's different.'

'So it might be. But...' I really was bellowing now. I'd seen Nig heading in my direction, and I wanted to talk to him privately, without an audience. Especially one that skipped around backwards. 'Just push off, will you, and give me a bit of peace.' I didn't watch her as she slipped away. Like I say, I'd had enough.

'Heard the news?' asked Nig, looking more cheerful than usual. 'We've got Friday off. The teachers are having one of their daft training days. I bet all they do is sit round drinking tea and moaning about us.'

'Yeah,' I said, rubbing my scar to remind him how tough I was. 'Friday off. Brilliant. What're we going to do?'

Even as I said the words, I felt sick. I'd been all set to miss the gang meeting this Saturday. After all, I had a ready-made excuse. 'Sorry, Nig. Can't make it. I've got to go to the dinosaur museum with my Dad.' But Friday was a whole new problem.

'Dunno yet,' said Nig. 'But I've told Mandy it's her turn to choose, so you'll probably need some spare cash with you. She's bound to want to play cards, and she always wins.'

I nodded helplessly. I'd seen the way Mandy could shuffle a pack of cards. She could also make them vanish into nowhere, then appear one by one between her fingers. It was tricky stuff, and I wouldn't have liked to play Snap with her, let alone some complicated gambling game.

'Fine,' I said. 'I'll ask my Mum for a bit of extra pocket money.' I was desperately trying to think of a good way out of all this.

Nig snorted. 'Why bother to ask? She's got a purse, hasn't she? Why don't you just help yourself? She'll never know. I'm always sorting through my Mum's bag, and she's never noticed yet.'

'Mine would,' I told him. 'She counts every penny. She's got more locks on her purse than they have for the Crown Jewels.' It was half true. Mum was always careful with her wages, because Dad hardly ever remembered to help her with the bills. But really, I just didn't like to think about taking her money. I mean, she works everso hard. And she trusts me. The idea of cheating her made my hands feel sweaty.

'Yeah,' Nig was saying. 'I suppose your Mum would have to be a bit clever with you around, wouldn't she?' He tapped his nose again. His look said, 'We all know you were put away when you were six. And we can guess what for.'

No one was more relieved than myself when the bell rang for lessons to start.

For the rest of that week, DD kept out of my way. At least, I didn't see her around, which came to the same thing. In a way, I missed her cheeky grin in the mornings, but I was glad of the chance to arrive at school in some sort of style. I took to wearing my jacket collar turned up all the time, and swaggering across the playground to meet the Parkers as if I'd known them all my life. Not that I wanted them as friends, but I didn't want them as enemies either, so I'd worked out that if I was with them they couldn't make a lot of rude remarks behind my back.

'Roll on Friday,' I used to chant whenever I saw them. I could never think of anything to say after that, but it was better than nothing. And I badly wanted to climb one step higher up the pecking order than Mandy. If I couldn't beat her, I'd never beat anyone.

Swimming was better than ever on Thursday. We were training for our life saving certificates, so we all had to wear our pyjamas over our swimsuits. It was dead funny. Nosy had so many stripes on his jacket that he looked like a walking deckchair, and Pam was covered in cuddly bunnies. We were all supposed to dive in and swim for a couple of laps, then take our clothes off while we trod water, but that's not as easy as it sounds. My trousers got so soggy and heavy I thought the elastic was going to snap, and when I tried to untangle myself I tied the legs in a knot. Even Handy Mandy had a spot of trouble unfastening her buttons with wet fingers, so you can see how difficult it was.

After that, we learned how to save people from drowning. Only we had to practise with footballs, because McAvity wouldn't let us borrow the beginners. He said it was too dangerous. Mind you, I think he nearly changed his mind when I asked for Nig. There had been a lot of splashing and arguing in the shallow end that day, and a trail of footprints already led back to the boys' changing room.

When the coach pulled up outside the school, McAvity gave us the traditional warning about crossing roads carefully and keeping away from railway tracks. I don't know why teachers always have to ramble on about zebra crossings just before a holiday. Perhaps it's some sort of law, and they get the sack if they don't do it. But it seems silly to me. I mean, children can get run over at any time, can't they?

Anyway, when he finally ran out of steam, we made a quick getaway and headed for home. We were free for three whole days, and most people couldn't wait to get started.

Nig strolled along with me. He had his collar turned up like mine and his hair was almost completely dry, but then, he'd been out of the water for longer than anyone else. 'See you in the morning,' he said when we came to my front door. 'Usual time, usual place. And don't forget the readies.' He licked his thumb and pretended to count a pile of ten pound notes.

'Yeah,' I said. 'See you.'

I was eating my tea, baked beans and a cheeseburger, when Gran started. 'Who was that on our doorstep this evening?'

'Nig,' I said through a mouthful of bun. 'My best

friend. I'm in his gang.'

'Well, you want to get out of it again.' Gran looked really grouchy as she whipped away my plate. I hadn't finished scraping up the tomato sauce yet. 'I don't like the look of that boy. Shifty eyes, if you ask me. He'll bring you nothing but trouble.'

'How can you tell?' I didn't like the way this was going. I was also a bit worried about my afters. 'You can't have seen him for more than a couple of seconds. And you haven't spoken to him at all.'

'Don't need to,' Gran yelled from the kitchen. I could hear her crashing saucepans and dishes around in the sink. The smell of burnt pastry wafted towards me. 'Wouldn't want to talk to him. I've told you. His middle name's Trouble.'

She thumped a dish down in front of me. A black pie sitting in a pool of yellow lumps. I was glad Gran didn't have bad moods too often.

'What happened to that nice little girl you were with the other day? I thought she was your best friend.'

I attacked one of the larger lumps with my spoon, but it fell back into the swamp. 'Don't be loopy,' I said. 'She's just a weedy little squirt.'

'So were you, not so many weeks ago,' said Gran, stumping back into the kitchen. 'And I'm not sure I didn't like you better that way.'

Jackie was in a rotten temper that evening too. She'd spent the entire week sketching stork-women, scribbling them out, and throwing the paper at Gran's china dog.

This monstrosity stood on the carpet guarding our TV and it was Gran's favourite ornament because Auntie Hat had bought it for her out of her first pay packet. Fluffer money. Mum says that Gran sat up in her dressing gown all that night, crying into her hanky, and when Auntie Hat stuck the dog's head round the door, she cried even more. Now the thing was called

Fluff, though Chips might have been more suitable, judging by the state of its ears. And it was half buried under a paper snowdrift.

'Having problems?' I asked. Unwisely.

'What does it look like?' Jackie let fly with her drawing arm and bounced a pencil sharpener off my ear. 'I've got to finish these designs by tomorrow and I haven't decided on the colours yet, let alone the main theme.'

I frowned over her shoulder at her latest effort. A long, floaty dress covered in purple spots. There were spikes all round the arm holes.

'Well, it's certainly different,' I said carefully. 'But you couldn't wear a coat over it, could you? Not unless you wanted to make holes in the sleeves. And you'd still end up looking like a porcupine with measles.'

Jackie pulled at her own hair with both hands and groaned. 'The idea is to choose one shape, and then just adapt it slightly so it could be worn almost anywhere. To the shops, to work, to a party...'

'Down the Tube,' I added. Quite helpfully, I thought. 'Squashed up on a train. Climbing the stairs. Queuing for tickets...' I looked again at the picture. 'No one could go to work in that. Every time they turned round, they'd stab someone. I reckon you'd be better off with something more comfortable, like Gran was telling you.'

Jackie laughed, but she didn't sound so scornful now. I suppose she was getting really desperate. 'Gran,' she said. 'What does she know about it?'

'I dunno. But you've got to admit, she's a good guesser. And you might as well give it a try.'

'Mmmm.' She still sounded doubtful, but she started to dig out her greens and browns, and across the top of a fresh sheet of paper she wrote, 'The Underground Collection. A series of designs in earthy shades, printed on natural fabrics for simplicity and comfort.'

Her pencil began to scrape away, so I left her to it and went off to find Mum. She had just got up, and was yawning over a plate of toast in the kitchen. Her dungarees were lying across a chair, ready to be packed in her work bag, and a half-finished shopping list lay on the table next to her purse.

'Mum,' I said in a drawn-out whine, to let her know that a question was coming. 'Can I have some extra pocket money tomorrow? Only I'm meeting the gang, and Nig says...'

'Sorry, love.' Mum took a gulp of tea and screwed up her face while the thick brew connected with her brain. 'I'm practically out of cash.' She pushed the list towards me. 'By the time I've bought that little lot, there won't be enough left to take my dungarees to the launderette.'

She smiled apologetically. I knew what she was thinking. If Dad had sent us a cheque last week, we'd have been all right.

'Never mind,' she said. 'I get paid tomorrow night. Ask me again on Saturday.'

I picked up the list. It was all important stuff, I could see that. Eggs, bread, milk, butter. 'I can get these for you,' I offered. 'I'm on holiday tomorrow. I could easily go round the shops for you.'

My face must have turned bright red. I didn't know where to look when she said, 'Oh, you are a good boy. That's everso thoughtful of you. It's a real treat to have you home and well.' Then she handed me her purse and I shoved the list inside it while she poured herself a second cup of tea.

The next morning I hurried downstairs with a purse-shaped bulge in my jacket pocket. After all, I was telling myself, it's not really stealing is it? I'm just borrowing the money to play cards with Mandy. Then I can buy Mum a present with my winnings when I do the shopping.

Jackie was still sitting at the living room table, and by the state of her hair I guessed she'd been drawing all night. The china dog was totally buried. As I walked in, she heaved herself up and shovelled a wodge of green and brown sketches into her college folder.

'Finished,' she announced in a muzzy voice. 'I'll have to rush. I'm late.' She snatched up a mug from the table and swallowed a mouthful of something black.

'Good luck,' I called after her as she dashed out of the door.

Two minutes later she came back, mumbled 'Thanks', and plonked the mug in my hands. Then she was gone again.

I poured myself a quick bowl of Krispy Krunchies, and ate them standing up. Jackie was right. It was late. Mum was already upstairs, sploshing about in the bath to wash off the Thursday night dust.

I shouted a general good-bye and was just about to leave the house, when Gran appeared at the bottom of the stairs like a small, grey ghost. For some reason, she had Jackie's newspaper cutting in her hand, and I could see the closing date of the competition circled in green and brown. It reminded me of the railway lines on a map of the Tube.

'Where are you going, young man?' she demanded.

'Just out with the gang.' I couldn't understand all the fuss. The piece of paper was quivering, and her hair looked as if she'd been sticking her fingers down an electric plughole. 'What's up Gran? Have you had one of your nightmares?' That would explain why she was so wild-eyed and frizzy.

She rubbed her hands over her face. 'Bombshell, bombshell,' she muttered. 'No. Not a nightmare exactly. More a bad dream. It was all muddled up with dark tunnels, and that friend of yours, and...' She made a sudden grab for me and shook me by the shoulders, as if this was a matter of life or death. 'You aren't going down the Underground again today, are you?' she asked. I was afraid she was going to burst into tears.

'Course not,' I told her. 'We did that last week. Everyone thought it was dead boring. Nig's got other plans for today.' Mum's purse felt like a lump of concrete over my heart, and I half expected Gran to notice it through my jacket.

But she didn't, because all she said was, 'That's all right then. I just don't want you going down there today. Please. Not today.'

'Why?' I asked. 'What's so special about today?'

She didn't answer. She just kept saying, 'Bombshell, bombshell,' over and over to herself, as if the word was stuck inside her head.

I squirmed out of her grip and opened the front door. 'Bye Mum,' I shouted. 'Bye Gran.' I couldn't get away fast enough.

The last thing I heard as I hurried down the street was a frantic little voice calling after me, 'And keep out of that boy's way. People who look for trouble generally end up finding it, you know.'

6
Looking for Trouble

I was hoping to reach the garage first for once. Then I could always say, 'Well, I waited for ages but no one came, so I gave up and went home.'

No chance. The Parkers and Mandy were already there, lighting matches and seeing who could hold on to the stick the longest. Nosy was sucking a scorch mark on his thumb.

'Oh no,' he said by way of a welcome. 'It's Super Scar. Got any more bright ideas, have you? Nice little trip round the knitting factory? Tea party with the vicar?'

'Not my turn,' I told him through my collar. 'Bet you can't think of anything better.'

'Bet I can,' said Nosy.

'Bet you can't.' My voice sounded funny. Sharp and squeaky, like a ventriloquist's dummy. What's more, I hadn't even moved my lips.

I whirled round, and there was DD doing my arguing for me. She looked really pleased with herself.

'What are you doing here?' I spluttered.

'Same as you,' she said. 'This is my gang too, remember.'

Nosy sneered at me, and I waited miserably for Pam to laugh. With fans like DD, who needed enemies?

'If it was my turn to choose, I'd go to the adventure playground,' she was telling everyone chirpily. 'We could have races up the rope ladders, and play dragon-hunts inside the big barrel.' She turned to Mandy. 'What would you do? Where would you like to take us?'

There was no answer of course. Mandy just pulled a toffee out of DD's ear, so Nosy chipped in instead.

'Well, I've got a better plan for a race. Supermarket trolleys. We nick them from the car park and take them down by the canal. First one in the water's a winner.'

DD scratched her head. 'Be a bit wet when we take them back,' she pointed out. 'They'll go all rusty.'

'Who said anything about taking them back?' Nosy burnt his thumb again in astonishment, and Pam hooted with pleasure. I'm not sure who had amused her the most.

'Shut up,' barked someone from the doorway. It was Nig, slouching in with his jacket tied round his waist by the arms, as if a very skinny wrestler was trying to hold him back. He sounded furious. 'Tough luck, Mandy. Card games are out. Got no cash.'

No one dared to complain in case that made him worse, so we all made sympathetic groaning noises.

'What happened to your Mum's handbag, then?' asked Pam. 'I thought you said you could always find a pound or two in there.'

Nig kicked one of the boxes against the garage wall, and the limp cardboard buckled forlornly. 'Dad got there first. He's gone and put it all on some stupid horse. Bongwell or Bow Bells or something. My Mum's going mad. There isn't a lousy penny in the house.'

I felt like laughing now. Loudly and hysterically. My glasses were starting to steam up with the relief. I'd be able to do Mum's shopping and take home the change as well. I wouldn't be in any trouble, and I wouldn't have to let anyone down. Best of all, I wouldn't have a guilty conscience. I'd even be able to prove Gran wrong. 'See. We just sat in Nig's garage and played Happy Families. Where's the harm in that?'

Someone nudged me roughly in the arm. It was Nig. 'You been listening?' he asked.

'Yeah,' I answered. 'What did you say?'

'We're going down the Underground again,' said DD excitedly. 'On our own. Without any grown ups.'

'And this time we won't just be looking for trouble,' said Pam and Nosy together. 'We'll be finding it.'

Mandy silently untied the torch and stowed it in her bag, which she hitched on her back to leave her arms free. The next minute, I was being jostled down the alleyway and along the pavement towards the station. I felt more like a prisoner than a member of the gang. I kept straining my neck to see if DD was still with us but Mandy always managed to block my view.

When we reached the Tube entrance Nig said, 'Remember. We're looking for chocolate machines, open handbags, wallets sticking out of back pockets. Anything like that. And thanks to Goggles here, we know all the back ways and short cuts, so if anyone starts shouting, just run for it.' He pressed his back against the stonework and waited until a crowd of foreign tourists flocked past.

'While they're paying for their tickets,' he whispered, 'we duck down so old Figgsy can't see us. Turn left and take the back stairs to platform three. See you there. And if you get caught, you're on your own.'

Only I wasn't on my own. I was arm in arm with Nig, skidding past the ticket office, dodging sideways, and scrambling past the 'No Entry' signs in breathless silence. I was glad I was feeling fitter these days, or I'd have probably ended up at the bottom of the stairs with a body full of smashed bones.

'Brilliant work,' said Nig warmly, when we reached the platform.

I leaned against a litter bin, panting noisily. 'What work?' I gasped.

'Sussing this place out for us. Finding all the hiding places. You're a genius.' He jerked his thumb towards Nosy, who had emerged out of one of the archways, and was now wedging a penknife into a chewing-gum dispenser while Pam stood guard. 'Don't mind them. Got no sense. Can't see ahead, like you and me.'

He was tapping his nose again. I wished he wouldn't. 'We're a great team, aren't we?' his eyes said. 'Nig the Boss and Goggles the Brains. A great team.'

'Yeah,' I said weakly. 'Have you seen DD yet?'

'Nah,' said Nig. 'But Mandy's busy. Look.'

I looked. Mandy was wandering dreamily down the platform, her face a complete blank. Every so often she would accidentally bump into someone and stagger away with a shrug while the other person apologized. A second later, she would slip something into her pocket. A slip of paper, a square of plastic, a small black object that looked like...

This was terrible. Surely someone would notice in a minute? I took off my glasses and rubbed them on my jeans. The world went soft and hazy. Fuzzy shapes floated around and bobbed against rubber walls, but as soon as I replaced my specs the true picture came back again. Bright and sharp and horribly clear.

'But that's stealing,' I hissed.

Nig stared at me. 'Course it's stealing,' he growled. 'What else did you expect? That was the whole point of coming down here in the first place, wasn't it?'

'No.' I sounded like some snivelly little first year, but I couldn't do anything about it. 'I just wanted to look round, that's all. I didn't want any...'

'Trouble?' Nig's eyes narrowed. 'Come off it, Goggles. You knew what we were looking for. And I always get what I want, don't I?'

'Well, yes,' I stammered. 'But this isn't right. You've got to stop them before the train comes. Make them give the stuff back.' I pointed desperately at Nosy and Pam, who were shaking white packets out of the slot machine. 'I'll buy them some chewing gum. I'll buy sweets for everybody. I've got plenty of cash.'

I felt for the purse, but my fingers were so trembly I couldn't find the right pocket. In any case, it wasn't my money. It was Mum's, and that meant I would be stealing too. So how could I criticize anyone else?

A deep rumble came from the far end of the tunnel and my eyes began to fill up. All those people would jump on the train, looking forward to a nice day round the shops. And as soon as the doors closed they would realize they'd been robbed. I had to warn them.

Nig grabbed me by the jacket and shoved me through one of the archways. 'I thought you were one of us,' he was snarling. 'You made out you were the big expert, didn't you? The big villain. Special school at six, and all that business.'

'No.' My lower lip was wobbling now and my nose had started to run. The noise of the train sounded like the roar of an ogre. Fee, Fi, Fo, Fum. Nig's fist was under my chin. 'It wasn't that sort of school. It was a boarding school for kids like me. I was ill, see? My heart wasn't working properly, so I couldn't go to an ordinary school. Not till after I had my operation.'

I rubbed my scar automatically, and the fist pressed my head back further.

'So it was a doctor who cut you open, was it?'

I tried to nod.

'You weren't in a fight at all?'

My head shook.

'What about all those stories you told us about your mates? That kid who was dying from smoking?'

'I didn't say that. I said he couldn't breathe sometimes. He had asthma. That's why the doctors told him cigarettes could kill him.'

'And that girl with the broken back. I suppose she didn't run under a train either?'

'No. She was in a road accident. Her school bus got smashed by a lorry.'

Nig nodded this time. Very slowly and deliberately, and he wasn't alone. Behind him I could see Mandy, Nosy and Pam, and I could hear the flick, flick, flick, of Nosy's penknife.

'Told you he was a creep, didn't I?' said Nosy. 'Told you we shouldn't let him in the gang.'

'Is he going to split on us?' Pam spat out. 'Is he going to blab to Figgsy?'

'I doubt that,' said Nig in his lowest growl. 'Because if he opens his mouth, I'm going to knock his teeth right down his throat.'

I closed my eyes. I was done for. If only I'd listened to Gran. If only I'd...

'Hey!' yelled a high squeaky voice. 'Look out, you lot. The police are coming. Figgsy saw you on the video screen, and he's rung the alarm.'

Nig dropped his fist and backed away from me as if I had the plague. 'Leave him,' he ordered. 'Follow me. Up the back stairs.'

The next moment a small hand snatched mine, and I was being towed along a winding passage full of scaffolding and chipped tiles. It looked vaguely familiar, but I didn't have time to admire the scenery.

'DD,' I gasped. 'Where did you spring from? How did you know about the police?'

'I didn't,' giggled my private fan club. 'I made it all up. Figgsy hasn't even got a video screen, has he? I don't remember seeing one.'

Now I came to think of it, I couldn't remember seeing one either. I only hoped Nig wasn't having the same thoughts, but I didn't like to say so. It might sound ungrateful, and DD had just saved my life. Well, my teeth, anyway.

'Where are we?' I asked. 'I'm completely lost now. I can't even remember where we started from.' I knew we had jumped over several 'Keep Out - Men at Work' signs, but everything else had been a confused blur.

The passage curved away in both directions, but one stretch of wall looked much the same as all the others once the new tiles had been fixed in place. No sprayed-on scribble, no dirty marks, no torn posters. Just smooth, clean whiteness. Distant rumblings shook the floor, but they didn't seem to come from any particular direction, unless it was under our feet.

The workmen must have knocked off for a cup of tea, because there was no one else around, so I stood in the shelter of some scaffolding and leaned back to recover from my fright. When I closed my eyes I could see splashes of purple and orange light, and the darkness under my lids spun like a crazy, electronic kaleidoscope.

'Gran told me not to come down here today,' I said. 'I should have listened to her. She's always right.'

'Grown ups usually are,' agreed DD. 'Makes you sick doesn't it?'

'Mmmm.' I leaned back further. It was nice to talk to someone who didn't scare me or make me feel small. I knew I ought to tell her I was sorry for being so mean to her at school, but instead I found myself saying, 'This bit of wall feels funny. All sort of soft and spongy.'

'It's the bricked-up archway,' said DD. 'They haven't tiled over it yet. They've left it all rough.'

'It doesn't feel rough,' I said. 'It feels like a heap of feathers.' I seemed to be sinking backwards, and my stomach was beginning to lurch. If I leaned just a fraction more I'd fall right over. I would disappear into the drifting softness and float away for ever.

I opened my eyes in panic. Was I fainting? I didn't feel dizzy, but maybe I was too weak to notice the usual clues. I reached out to grab the cool, metal poles and pull myself upright.

'DD,' I said hoarsely. 'Let's get out of here. I think I need some fresh air.' There was a thumping noise inside my head now, and I was sure the scaffolding had begun to vibrate. For a second, she grinned at me. Then her face went serious too, and her hand slithered damply into mine. I didn't mind. I was glad of the company.

'They're coming back,' she whispered, pointing to our right. 'They'll turn us into mincemeat if they catch us this time.'

She was right. The thumping noise was getting louder. Heavy feet were thundering towards us along the stony corridors, and the booming we could hear wasn't a train. It was Pam. 'Get the creeps! Get the creeps!' The echo found us and surrounded us. 'Creeps! Creeps! Creeps!'

This was the end. Or at least, it was the end for me. I couldn't outrun the Garage Gang on the best of days, and now my shoes seemed to have glued themselves to the floor. 'Run for it, DD,' I croaked. But she only tightened her grip on my fingers.

'Can't,' she said, pointing to our left. 'The workmen are coming back as well.' In the distance I could hear men's voices singing an old pop song. Any minute now, they would turn the corner and find us. Two kids with no tickets. Trespassers in a forbidden area. There'd be prosecutions, fines, big trouble. What could I do? What could I do? I closed my eyes again and sank back against the brickwork with a whimper.

And before I could stop myself, I was plunging through a whirlwind of cold air that sucked me down and down, until I thudded against something warm and alive. It was swearing. And it seemed to be wrapped in a blanket

7
Beyond the Archway

DD's hand still hung on to mine as we rolled away from the bundle of grey wool.

'What the hell?' protested a voice, half asleep and half furious. 'Look where you're going, can't you? Clumsy idiots. Can't you see this section's booked? Go and find your own pitch. And mind where you're treading.'

It was a young man, tightly wrapped in a cocoon of bedding. His head was resting on a canvas bag, and there was something about his stubbly chin that rang bells inside my head. I wondered whether his teeth were perfectly straight, and whether he had bright pink gums, but I couldn't see. He had pulled a blue cap over his eyes and he was pretending to be asleep again.

Behind us I thought I could hear more angry complaints, muffled and very far away. 'Lost them... Can't have... Which way?'

'Quick,' I whispered to DD. 'It's the gang. If they follow us through the bricks, they'll...' I looked back the way we had come and stifled a scream. The wall had vanished. It simply wasn't there.

In its place was a curved archway, leading out into an empty passage. Except that it wasn't quite empty. Hovering in the air, twisting and shaking, was the ghostly shape of a head. Just the back of it. I could see the stumpy neck, and the red rims of the ears.

'It's Nig,' squealed DD excitedly, as if this was some sort of wild party game. 'He'll fall through in a minute. Look!'

The head had been joined by a pair of broad shoulders, and hovering beside them was the squashed point of a nose. I'd seen it plenty of times before, mainly behind steamy windows at school.

'Nosy,' I groaned. This was as bad as a late night horror show. I wanted to run, but I wanted to stay and watch at the same time.

'Can't you see them?' I asked the man in the blanket, but he muttered something rude and pulled his cap further down over his eyes. At the same moment there came a faint cry from the other world.

'Oi! You kids! What d'you think you're doing? Keep away from the scaffolding. It's going to...' Somewhere, a metal pole crashed to the ground, but the noise was so soft it could have been happening on another planet.

'I wouldn't stay there if I were you,' I warned the blue cap. 'Any minute now...'

But it was too late. In an explosion of swear words, Nig came plummeting into the tunnel and sprawled across the man's legs, closely followed by Nosy, whose face crunched into a pair of empty boots.

'Woff goind onf?' he bleated, heaving himself up out of the smelly leather and staring at my knees.

'I'm not sure,' I said. 'Look out. Here comes Pam. And Mandy.'

The girls arrived shoulders first, and at great speed. They careered past us, trampled on someone who was quietly snoring inside a sleeping bag, then trampled back again.

'Gawd,' said Pam, picking bits of powdered tile out of her hair. 'That was close. I thought we'd had our chips. The whole lousy lot was coming down.' She pointed her foot at the sleeping bag, which had snuffled and turned over. 'What's all this then? Didn't know beggars were allowed down here.'

'Watch your tongue, my girl.' The man in the blue cap sat up and began stuffing his boots into his bag. 'Don't have beggars at this station. And well you know it.' His pillow looked horribly lumpy now, and I couldn't imagine how he was ever going to sleep on it.

'What d'you think you're playing at?' he carried on. 'Should have been in bed hours ago. Clear off. Find your Mums. And you can tell them from me, there's big trouble if you disturb us again.'

The snorer gave a powerful grunt and sat up. 'Get out of it!' he yelled at us. 'Little perishers. Who do you belong to? Shouldn't be in London anyway. Should be miles away, if your parents had any gumption.'

'What do you mean?' I stammered out. I was beginning to feel as if I'd stepped into someone else's bad dream. One that was all muddled up with dark tunnels, and Nig, and...

'Why shouldn't we be in London? It's our home,' DD finished for me. She had let go of my hand and was fussing round Nosy instead.

'Home?' The snorer laughed nastily. 'If you're lucky. If it hasn't been flattened by the time you get out of here in the morning. Your family should have had you evacuated, like all the rest of the kids.'

'What's he on about?' demanded Nig, unknotting his jacket and putting it on. 'Why's everyone lying on the floor? It's only about twelve o'clock.'

'That's right.' The snorer jabbed his finger at a green alarm clock which sat beside him on a folded towel. 'Almost midnight. And some of us have to start work at six tomorrow. So for gawd's sake...'

'Ssssh!' hissed a woman further down the passageway. 'Some of us need our beauty sleep, you know.'

Now I saw that the entire tunnel was carpeted with bulgy grey shapes. Human bodies, lying side by side like seals on a beach, and grumbling through open yawns. It made me think of a picture I had seen recently, in a book at school. People just like this, heaped up on a wooden escalator.

I swung round. DD was mopping blood off Nosy's top lip with her hanky, while Mandy stood and stared at the ground. The bag on her back made her look like a bored camel. Pam stabbed angrily at the empty space where the brick wall should have been.

'I've got the jitters,' Nig growled down my ear. 'Let's get out of here.'

'Out of where?' asked DD happily. 'It's like an old movie, isn't it?'

'Mmmm,' I said. 'Very old. About fifty years, if you ask me.'

'Doesn't matter how old. You got us into this, so you can get us out again.' Nig was starting to sound a bit frantic.

'I can't,' I told him. 'I don't even know how it happened. All I know is, we've walked into an Underground air raid shelter. And I think we're in the middle of the London Blitz.'

I'd hardly finished speaking when a distant boom shuddered downwards, and a spray of dust stung our eyes. Even Mandy coughed. Pam threw her whole body at the missing brickwork and catapulted herself straight through the archway. It was a wasted effort. She wandered back again with her mouth open and her face full of questions.

'You're making a draught,' grumbled the man with the blue cap. He pulled his blanket over his head and settled himself down to sleep again. I had a feeling he must be somewhere near the bottom of the pecking order, because his bed was in such a chilly spot. It couldn't be far from the surface either. If a bomb ever happened to land on the ticket office...

'Where's the safest place?' I asked.

His hand wriggled out of the bedding and pointed down the crowded tunnel.

'Follow me,' I said. I gave Nig's sleeve a tug, then began to pick my way over and round the bodies. They were mostly women, but there were a few men, either very old or very young. One or two wore uniforms and I saw a young soldier with his arm in a sling. He was cuddling it as if it were a wounded animal.

'Hurry up, you little devils,' he said in a friendly way. 'There's a raid on up there you know. Your mothers must be worried sick. Then he squinted at Nosy. 'You're a Parker, aren't you?' he asked.

'Yeah,' said Nosy, sniffing into DD's hanky. 'So what if I am?'

'Nothing,' said the man. 'Just thought I recognized the nose from somewhere.' He jerked his good thumb towards the archway on our left. 'Your lot are down there, aren't they? That's usually the Parker pitch.'

'Yeah,' I said quickly. 'That's right. That's where we always sleep.' And I shot round the corner.

'What's the big hurry?' whined Nig. 'I want to get out of here. You're leading us further in.'

'I know,' I whispered. 'But what else can we do? We can't keep drawing attention to ourselves, or someone's going to notice our clothes. We're lucky they've all been half asleep so far.'

'Lucky?' Nig didn't sound exactly convinced. 'What's so lucky about it? We want to get back to the garage and have a look at all Mandy's loot.'

'Yeah,' agreed Pam and Nosy together. 'Where's the back stairs?'

'This way,' I said in my best Jack-the-Lad voice. I didn't really have the foggiest idea, but perhaps if we could find a platform we might be able to work out an escape route. But to where? Another boom rang through the maze of tunnels, and we all ducked instinctively. I, for one, didn't fancy climbing any closer to that sort of danger.

'Come on,' I called back over my shoulder, but before I could move, a cold hand seized my ankle and I gasped with terror. I couldn't help it. The winding passages were starting to feel spooky, and I half expected to meet Dracula round every turning.

When I looked down, I saw that the fingers belonged to a tiny girl in a pink dressing gown. She was sound asleep, and must have mistaken my socks for a passing teddy bear. I stooped to unpeel her grip as gently as I could without waking her. There was a letter 'H' embroidered across her top pocket, and she whistled softly as she breathed out.

'Mind where you're going,' I whispered to the others. 'Don't stand on anyone.'

We threaded our way past a woman who was probably the girl's mother, then I grinned with relief as a wave of cool air struck my face. An airway. We must have reached a Tube platform at last. I wasn't sure how much good it would do us, but at least we wouldn't be lost any more.

'Shift yourself, Goggles,' grumbled Pam. 'This place smells like the boys' toilets at school. They never tell you about that in the history books, do they?'

'Yeah,' agreed Nosy through the hanky. 'It stinks.'

Then it happened. An almighty boom, louder than anything we had heard before. Dust and chunks of brick came raining down on us, and two hands grabbed at mine. One I knew only too well. It was DD's. The other was big, rough and trembling. Surely it couldn't be Nig's?

'My gawd,' growled a voice. 'We're gonna die.'

All around us people were screaming, and a roaring noise clogged my ears.

'It's a train,' Nosy was yelling. 'We're all gonna be flattened.'

'Don't be daft,' I shouted back. 'It can't be. It's too late. And in any case, we're nowhere near the rails.' But the roaring was coming closer and even though it was impossible, I began to think he must be right.

The worst of it was, we didn't know which way to run. No one did. Women were jumping up and clutching at their blankets. Children were sobbing. The little girl was clinging to her mother, and we were being pushed in all directions as people tore past us in panic.

'Which way?' wailed Nig. 'I don't like this.'

'Cheer up,' I told him. 'You wanted trouble, and we've certainly found it.' But my brain was spinning too, and even my feet felt numb. The crush and the noise were getting to me, and I just wanted to curl up in a tight ball until the whole thing was over. After all, it was only a nightmare, wasn't it? Like one of those stories we were always writing for McAvity. You know. '...And then I woke up and it was all a dream.'

'Quick, Goggles! Quick!' It was DD, hauling frantically at my sleeve. 'We've got to find the train tunnel. We've got to find our way out of here before it's too late.'

I suddenly realized why my feet had gone dead. They were freezing cold. Thick torrents of black water were swirling round them and sweeping us sideways.

'It's a flood,' squawked Nig. 'Oh my gawd. I can't swim.' He clamped my wrist so tightly I thought he was going to stop the blood.

'Come on, then,' I shouted. 'Follow DD.'

But he didn't budge. He just stood there shaking, while the waves smacked into him, and other people's belongings hurtled between his legs.

'Push him,' I yelled at the Parkers and Mandy. 'Pick

78

him up and drag him. Otherwise we'll all drown.'

Then we were skidding and sliding and stumbling down the corridor towards the draught of cold air that could save our lives. People stampeded past us with their arms full of bedding, and I shrieked at the top of my voice, 'This way. Please. Follow us!'

But either they couldn't hear me or they wouldn't listen, because no one joined us, and all the time the water was getting deeper and fiercer. At any moment we were going to be lifted up and carried away, whether we wanted it or not. The ceiling seemed very close now, as if it was squeezing down on us, and I raked at the water with my hands to pull myself along.

By the time we reached the platform, the railway itself had become a river. We hurtled out of the tunnel and over the edge like sticks at a waterfall, and I heard Nig's cry of terror behind me as I surfaced. I struck out blindly until I caught a handful of thick material. I didn't know whose collar it was, but I knew I had to hang on, whatever happened, or I'd never forgive myself.

'Grab my leg,' a thin voice was calling. 'Hold on, Goggles.'

A foot hit me in the eye and I snatched at it with my free hand. I was being pulled in half. I was going under. Life-saving lessons in the pool had never been like this. My shoes and my jacket felt like sacks of cement.

I can't say the whole of my life flashed before me, but I definitely saw Gran's face. 'Don't go down the Underground today,' she was saying. 'People who look for trouble... Bombshell, bombshell... Where's that nice little girl?'

'It's me.' DD's grin was like a strange, curved moon looking down at me from a curved stone sky. 'The waves threw me up on these bunk beds. We've got you and Nig. We're just waiting for Nosy.'

Pam and Mandy, both soaked to the skin, sat dripping beside her. Nig was flat out on his back, still gasping and blowing bubbles. A beached fish in a soggy anorak.

'My Gran,' I started to say, 'is too clever by half...'

But a swearing, splashing, kicking body was heading towards us, and the girls leaned over to grab Nosy's belt.

'Climb up the side of the bunks,' Pam ordered him. 'We all managed it easy-peasy.'

That did the trick. Nosy was soon squelching up to join us on the top bunk, his hair hanging in strings. But nothing was easy here. Not really. We were all shivering and close to tears as we sat watching the torrent of water. It wasn't slowing down. If anything, it was getting deeper. Soon it would sweep the bunks away too.

'Now what?' I said. Pam was wringing out her hair over my arm, but I was too wet to care.

'We catch the baby,' said a voice I didn't recognize. It was quiet, calm and extremely snooty. It should have belonged to the sort of person you see on TV comedy shows about rich people in big houses. Only it didn't. It belonged to Mandy, who was busily unstrapping her bag from her back.

I nearly fell off my perch in surprise, but this was no time for fooling about. Swirling below us into the mouth of the Tube, along with all the shelter debris, the toys and the books and the handbags, was a small, relaxed bundle. A tiny girl floating on a sleeping bag. Air must somehow have been trapped inside it, and because she was so light it was holding her up. But for how much longer?

I thought of the deep, twisting tunnels that Jack the Lad had described to us, and I knew we would have to act quickly. I slithered back down the side of the bunks with Mandy, and reached out while she held my jacket. The sleeping bag spun in the current, but just as it slid into the great opening I managed to catch one corner.

DD gave a shout of pleasure as I hauled the flimsy raft closer and lifted the baby free. Then the bag was sucked away, and we watched it disappear into the black hole. I felt limp all over. The baby struggled against my chest and started to grizzle.

'Give her to me,' said Mandy. She stretched out her hands, and I couldn't help remembering how skilfully they could shuffle cards or steal the belongings from a tourist's pocket. Maybe that had all been practice for this moment. Maybe...

'Poor little scrap,' she was saying, as she carried the child back to the top bunk. 'Don't you worry. We'll soon find your Mummy and Daddy for you. Auntie Mandy's here now.'

I followed, and flopped between her and Nig. 'Why?' I asked her. 'Why didn't you ever speak before?'

Mandy pulled a face. 'Because my voice doesn't fit. I'd get teased all day long, wouldn't I? And anyway...' She rubbed the little girl's hands between her own to warm them up. 'I didn't have anything I wanted to say.'

I nodded. I thought I understood.

DD and I shook Nig and made him sit up. He coughed out a mouthful of water and hung his head over his knees.

'We've got to go,' DD told him. 'If the flood gets any higher, we could still drown.' A powerful jet was gushing out of the archway, as if someone had left a giant tap running at full force.

'Water main must have busted,' said Nosy, shaking his head gloomily. A drip fell off his nose and soaked into the blanket. 'That could keep going for days.'

Pam nodded. 'Days,' she said. 'We should know. Our Dad's a plumber.'

'OK,' I said. 'So which way do we go? Up the stairs to the street? Or along the track to the embankment?'

'What's the choice?' moaned Nig. 'I'll never make it

anyway. I'm finished.'

'Well, I don't fancy the stairs,' said Pam, ignoring him. 'Not after all those bombs. If the exit's been blocked, we could get half way up and find ourselves trapped. No thanks.'

'No thanks,' echoed Nosy, shaking another drip off his nose.

'The railway, then?' I asked.

Mandy nodded. She had been checking through the contents of her bag. One pack of cards, rather stuck together. Three oranges, good as new, which she juggled to make the baby smile. One sad-looking bunch of paper flowers. And the garage torch. She flicked it on, and by some miracle it still worked. We could just make out the orange circle as it swooped into the tunnel at the opposite end of the platform.

'It's impossible,' moaned Nig again. 'Look at the speed of the water. No one's going to get through that.'

I didn't want to admit it, but I could see he was right. The current was simply too strong. Fighting against it wouldn't just be stupid. It would be suicidal.

'Don't worry,' said DD, as cheerfully as ever. 'We'll be all right. Goggles is bound to think of something in a minute.' And she treated me to one of her adoring gazes.

'For crying out loud,' I wanted to shout. 'I'm not Superman. I'm just a weedy kid with glasses.'

But there wasn't time. A fourth, terrible explosion shook the air, and we clung to the bunks with all our strength, praying that they wouldn't fall to pieces or throw us into the murderous river. All around us we could hear massive crashes and rumbles, which shuddered on and on for what felt like hours. Then at last they died away, and we plucked up the courage to open our eyes.

The worst had happened. Our whole world had turned black.

8
The Tunnel

We were in total darkness. Not the sort of dark you get in your bedroom at night, when you can still see shadows and the ghostly shape of your dressing gown on the door. This was more like being locked in a black, velvet box.

'Oh gawd.' That was Nig. 'What're we going to do now?'

'Use the torch, of course,' said Mandy. She sounded snootier than ever, but no one bothered to comment. We waited for the soft click of the switch, and breathed out together as soon as we saw each other in the weak orange glow.

The little circle of light bounced across the roof and along the station walls like a lost star, and the baby began to gurgle happily. Perhaps she thought she had seen a golden butterfly floating by. Mandy swung the beam towards the archway, and DD squealed with excitement.

'The water! It's stopped. The bomb must have stopped it.'

I peered through my splashed lenses. She was right. Instead of an open entrance there was now a wall of broken bricks, and the torrent had become a thin, gleaming trickle.

'We can make it,' I said. 'But we'll have to be quick. The blockage can't hold the water back for long.'

'I'm not going down any tunnels.' Nig was shaking so much, I could feel the bunks wobbling. 'You heard what that old bloke told us last week. We'll go the wrong way. We'll end up miles underneath London, and we'll never get out alive.'

'It can't be all that bad,' I told him. 'Not if my Mum can do it. She gets lost if you spin her round in the supermarket.'

DD began to wriggle herself along to the edge of the bunk. 'We could use the bed clothes,' she said. 'We could knot the sheets together and make a sort of rope. Then we could hang on to it and we wouldn't lose each other. Like in my story book at school. There's this man in a maze, and he unravels a ball of wool, and...'

'Mmmm,' I said doubtfully, prodding the soaked blankets. 'It's a clever idea, but wet sheets would be far too heavy. What we need is string.'

'Or flags.' We all turned to squint at Mandy. She was digging around in her top pocket, and the next minute she began to fling out an endless line of coloured bunting. 'It's one of my best tricks,' she explained proudly. 'It goes on for about half an hour.' DD clapped her hands, and the baby blew a large bubble.

'Brilliant,' I said, catching the first few triangles and winding them round my waist. 'Let's go. Mandy first, because she's got the torch and the flags and the baby. Everyone agreed?'

'Yeah,' said Pam. 'But if the water starts rising again, she'll have to go on by herself and get help.'

'Fine by me,' said Mandy. 'Here goes.' She swung herself over the side and dropped down to the platform. The flood still came almost to her waist, but it was calm now, so she could wade along easily. We watched her move away, trailing more and more flags behind her as she went. What with the hump of her bag at the back, the baby zipped into her anorak at the front, and the wavering torchlight, she looked like an alien from outer space. The Man-Eating Blob from Mars.

Pam was next, sliding her fingers along Mandy's magic rope and feeding it back to us. Then Nosy. This was beginning to feel like an elephant act at the circus, with everyone linking trunks and tails, only a circus would have had bright spotlights and music. This place was horribly quiet, as if it was waiting to erupt again without warning. And it was getting darker all the time, as the torch moved further and further away.

'Oh gawd,' Nig was moaning. 'Oh gawd. Oh gawd.'

'You're next,' I said to DD. 'Go as fast as you can. We may not have much longer.' I sounded so confident you'd have thought I did this sort of thing every day, but underneath my scar, my heart was turning somersaults.

'You go without me,' whimpered Nig. 'I'm not moving. I'm staying here.'

'Don't be daft,' I said. 'You can't. It's too dangerous. And in any case, everyone's waiting for you.' I could feel the flags tugging at my waist. Somebody was getting impatient.

There was a noisy sploshing below us. 'Hurry up,' shouted Nosy. 'I can hear the bricks groaning. I'm not waiting much longer.'

Mandy aimed the torch at us, and I could just see Nig's face. It was stiff with fear, and even in the soft glow it seemed to be turning green.

'Go on,' I said to DD again. 'Go without us. We'll catch you up.'

But she wouldn't move. She gripped my arm and shook her head. 'No. Not without you and Nig. You're my friends.'

I could hear Nosy splashing away. This was no time for gentle persuasion or reasoned arguments. 'Look,' I yelled at Nig, hauling him up by the collar. 'If you don't follow DD this minute, I'll...I'll...'

I knew what I was expected to say. I knew what I was supposed to do. I even lifted up my fist and held it under his chin. But I couldn't punch Nig's frightened face, not even to save my life. It was DD who came to my rescue, as usual.

'I'll give you a great big sloppy kiss right on the lips,' she told him triumphantly. 'And the last one off this bunk's a chicken.' With that she was gone, and Nig was scrambling after her so fast I could hardly keep up with him.

He soon slowed down. Ploughing through the water was hard for all of us. DD was tiny, Nig was terrified and I was tired, but we had to make it somehow. So we towed ourselves along the guideline, and kept close together as we struggled past the bulging bricks of the archway. Then we followed the torch beam to the far end of the platform, where the others were waiting for us.

'What took you so long?' asked Mandy, as Pam and Nosy got ready to swim into the tunnel.

'Oh, nothing,' I said, handing her a huge bundle of soggy flags. I had tried to coil them up neatly, but they would never fit into her pocket again, I was sure of that. 'I just had to tie my shoelaces, that's all.'

She nodded, and a gigantic shadow on the wall waggled its monstrous head. The baby began to chuckle. I suppose it felt safe and warm, but the rest of us certainly didn't. There was a sinister rumbling behind the broken bricks now, and the thin trickle had already grown to a steady stream.

'Let's go,' I said. 'I'll help Nig, if the rest of you can help Mandy.'

The Parkers dived together, and bobbed up again quickly. 'It's not very deep,' spluttered Pam. 'The water's running in the other direction. We must be going uphill.'

Mandy squeezed out the flags, stuffed them inside her bag, then handed the whole lot to Pam. She gave the torch to Nosy. 'You carry these,' she told the twins. 'If I swim on my back, the baby won't even get wet.' To prove it, she launched herself into the tunnel and pulled smoothly away.

'Will you be all right?' I asked DD.

'Yep,' she said. 'I can do doggy paddle. I'm a good swimmer.' And she threw herself noisily after the others.

Nig didn't move. He didn't even seem to be breathing. He just hung on to my arm and gulped a lot.

'You must think I'm a rotten lousy coward,' he said at last. 'I can't swim and I'm scared of the dark. I'm really pathetic.'

'No you're not,' I told him. 'You're brave. You're the bravest person here.'

'Oh, very funny,' he said with a sniff. 'Ha lousy ha.'

'I'm not joking,' I told him. 'It's true. It's been easy for the rest of us because we all love swimming, and I've always liked being in the dark. But you climbed off the bunk even though you were really scared. That makes you a proper hero, doesn't it?'

'I dunno. Does it?' Nig was gulping again. He knew what he would have to do next.

'OK,' I said, as calmly as I could. I ached all over and I wasn't feeling particularly energetic. 'Lean back, and I'll hold you round the chest so your head doesn't go under. We'll be fine if you can just relax.'

'Oh yeah,' groaned Nig. 'Just relax. Fine. Nothing to it.'

But he let me support him, and when I leaned backwards to balance on the water he managed not to struggle. I pushed hard against the flow with my legs and forced my eyelids open. I thought I could make out the shadowy curve of the ceiling, and further up the tunnel there was a muddle of voices shouting encouragement.

'Keep going, Goggles. Don't panic, Nig. Not far now. It's shallow once you get round the corner.'

My shoulder thumped against solid stone, and for the second time that day friendly hands guided me to safety. I raised my head to push myself upright and Nig toppled forward with a yelp. Then he shouted with relief.

'I'm standing up. It's all right. We did it.'

'Not quite,' said Mandy. 'There's a choice of two tunnels. And the torch battery's going flat.'

'Your fault,' Pam grumbled at Nosy. 'You must have got it wet.'

'No I didn't. I held the handle in my teeth. Anyway, it wouldn't be working at all if it was full of water, would it?'

'Shut up,' said Mandy. The baby was hiccuping now and, judging by the funny smell, it was going to need its nappy changed pretty soon. 'We haven't got much longer before the light goes out. Which way do we go? Left or right?'

'Right,' I said. 'Because it feels draughtier and that means fresh air. Anyway, I don't want to cross the track in case the lines are still alive.'

'I think we'd be dead already if they were,' said Pam. 'Our Dad says electricity can travel through water.'

'Yeah,' said Nosy. 'He learned that in his plumbing exams.'

There was a general nodding of heads, but we all pressed ourselves against the damp wall to be on the safe side. Mandy took the flags out of her bag again, and handed one end to me.

'You go first this time,' she said. 'I'll fix the other end to these pipes.'

I waited for her to make a knot round the thick service cables, then I set off. I don't know whether I looked fearless, but my legs were all weak and trembly inside my trousers, and my lenses were so spotty I felt as if I was burrowing through a plum pudding.

'Isn't this exciting, Goggles?' DD nattered happily behind me. 'Much better than the boring old adventure playground.'

'Glad to hear it,' I muttered ungratefully. 'Have I gone blind, or...?'

'The light's gone,' shouted Mandy. 'I can't make it work at all.'

'Oh gawd,' moaned a familiar voice. 'Oh gawd. How much further?'

We stumbled on, tripping over all sorts of strange lumps and bumps, or colliding with each other by accident. Everyone was grumbling at everyone else, and we were all losing our tempers.

'Look where you're going, can't you?'

'No I can't, stupid.'

'Stupid yourself.'

And so on, and so on, always keeping as close as we could to the tunnel wall. The route snaked in all directions, and soon it was impossible to tell whether we were going backwards, forwards or simply round in circles. My head was spinning and my bundle of flags was getting smaller and lighter, but I told myself we would be all right as long as we kept on trudging uphill. Which was quite a comforting thought, until I crashed into something lumpier and harder than anything we had met so far.

'We're lost, aren't we?' wailed Nig. 'I knew it. It's a dead end, isn't it? We'll all have to turn round and go back to the start. And the flood will come up the tunnel, and we'll all be drowned, and...'

'It's a dead end all right,' I said, dumping the flags on

the ground. 'But I think it must be fresh. It feels like a pile of broken stones. The roof must have caved in here as well.'

'We're trapped,' Nig began again. 'We're all gonna...'

'Hey,' Nosy said to him. 'I can see your rotten face. You've been blubbing, haven't you?'

I took off my filthy glasses and rubbed them on my sleeve. Without them, the world was actually clearer. I could see five grey shapes behind me, and a small point of light sparkling above my head.

'It's a star!' yelled DD. 'We're at the end of the tunnel. All we've got to do is get out.'

'Oh yeah.' Nig slid down the wall and slumped in a dejected heap. 'That's all we've got to do. Shift a lousy avalanche with our bare hands and get out.'

The rest of us slithered down to join him. We were all exhausted, and none of us felt exactly hopeful. Except for DD, of course.

'Cheer up,' she said. 'We're bound to be all right, aren't we? Because we know we're going to be alive in fifty years time. See?'

I frowned. I wished I could be so sure. 'I don't know,' I said. 'Maybe we'll just be reported missing, and no one will ever find us again. The papers are always printing mystery stories about people who go out for a walk and disappear for ever.'

'Yeah,' said Pam. 'Perhaps that's because they all lean against magic walls and pop through into the old days.'

'Yeah,' agreed Nosy. 'Into the old days. Creepy stuff.'

'Oh gawd,' said Nig. 'Pack it up. You're making me worse.' Then he leapt to his feet with a squawk.

'What is it?' I asked. 'Sorry, I didn't mean to upset you.'

'You didn't.' Nig's teeth were chattering now. 'It was a rat. A lousy great rotten rat. It ran right over my legs.'

'Oh,' I said. 'A mouse probably. My Mum sees lots of them down here. It's their home. She says they're quite cute really.'

'Quite cute?' Nig was shouting. 'Quite cute? What's the matter with you? Doesn't this place bother you at all?'

'Not much,' I admitted. It felt like a guilty secret. 'I can't help it. I think I must take after my Mum. She comes from a long line of Fluffers, you know. There's Gran, and my Auntie Hat...'

The baby started to squall loudly and we all held our ears.

'Someone else can give her a cuddle,' said Mandy. 'My arms are dropping off.'

I reached out and took the little bundle. The face was ugly now, all scrunched up and hot with crying, but there was something about it that I recognized.

'It's the little girl who grabbed my leg,' I said. 'Before the flood started. I remember her dressing gown, because it's got an 'H' on the pocket.'

No one was listening. They were all too keen to get away from the baby. The noise and the smell were working wonders on their weary brains.

'How about a human pyramid?' said Nosy. 'We could all stand on each other's shoulders, and shove the kid through the top.'

'We can't do that,' said DD. 'We'll hurt her. But I bet I could get out dead easy. I'm only little, and I can climb trees. I'm a good climber.'

'Are you sure?' I asked. 'Do you really want to try it?'

'Yep. I told you, I know we're going to be all right.'

I shrugged. It wasn't a brilliant plan, but it was the only one we had. 'OK,' I said. 'Who's going to make the base?'

Nig, Pam and Mandy rammed their heads together and laced arms to form a tight huddle, while I set

91

Baby H carefully down next to the wall. She was still crying, on and off, but she was too sleepy to crawl very far. Then I clambered up to kneel on Nig's shoulders. Nosy joined me, and we gripped each other's collars, making an unsteady platform between us.

'Good luck, DD,' I called. 'I think we're ready. Give it a whirl.'

Her hands and feet were everywhere at once. Pulling my hair, trampling over my back, sticking down my neck.

'Gerroff,' Nosy was bellowing. 'You're breaking my ears off.'

'Stand still. You're too bouncy. I can't reach,' DD answered. Then her heels pushed down, the pyramid collapsed and the light vanished, all at the same time. When we untangled ourselves, I looked up to see a pair of blurred legs wriggling through the opening. Then the star shone again.

'It's the embankment,' we heard her shout. 'I can see lots of people. And a train. I told you we were going to be all right, didn't I?'

Baby H hugged my ankle and howled more furiously than I would have believed possible. She might have been sore and tired and hungry, but there was definitely nothing wrong with her lungs.

9
All-clear

Other voices joined DD's. Adult voices, shouting words of encouragement to us and instructions to each other.

'Don't panic, kids. Help's on its way. We'll soon get you out of there.'

'Watch it, Bill. Take it easy, Jack. Pass us the crowbar, someone. All together now. Heave.'

The stones creaked and shifted. A woman warned us to stand well back and cover our eyes. Chips of cement rattled across the rails, and the small opening grew steadily larger as the barricade disintegrated. But above all the hammering and confusion, I could still hear DD laughing and chattering. 'I told them we'd be all right. I knew Goggles would get us out. He's my best friend, you know.'

We waited with our backs against the wall and watched the moonlight gradually seep in through the widening gaps. We knew we were filthy and bedraggled, but we felt terrific. We had beaten the air raid. We had beaten the flood. We had beaten the underground maze. Only Baby H sounded sorry for herself, and she was too young to know any better.

'Thanks,' Nig whispered in my ear. 'I couldn't have made it without you.'

'Course you could,' I said, jiggling the baby in my arms. 'Everyone's braver than they think. And anyway, it was all my fault in the first place. If I hadn't fixed up that visit last week...'

'No,' said Nig. 'It was my fault. If I hadn't made you go back to the station today...'

'No. My fault. I ran off with DD and fell through the wall...'

'No. My fault. I chased after you and...'

'Pack it up, you two. You're standing on my flags.' Mandy elbowed us out of her way and picked up the tangled bunting. Then she gave the long end of the string a sideways tug and began reeling it in.

'How did you manage that?' I asked, forgetting my squabble with Nig. 'I saw you tie it to the cables.'

'Conjuror's slip-knot,' she said proudly. 'My father taught me. Now watch this.' She was folding the triangles together at lightning speed, so they lay almost flat on the ground. I put on my glasses, took them off, wiped them on my sleeve and hooked them over my ears again, but I still couldn't see how she did it.

'Magic,' said Nig admiringly.

'Yep,' said Mandy. 'That's what you're supposed to think.' And giving us a slow wink, she replaced the neat parcel in her top pocket.

'OK, kids,' called somebody in an American accent. 'Get ready. We're coming through.'

I hurriedly stuck my glasses in my pocket and waited for the final flurry of grit. The great lumps of brick and concrete shifted upwards, then crashed back and rolled to one side. The tunnel was open. We were free.

The others edged past me, stepping cautiously over the buckled rails and the loose rubble. 'Take it easy,' the American said kindly. 'How many have we got? Anyone injured? Are you all safe?'

'Yes,' I heard Mandy saying. 'We're fine. There's six of us. And the baby, of course.'

'Baby? What baby?' A woman was speaking now.

Anxiously, as if she was about to burst into tears.

'Baby H,' I said, stumbling forwards to meet the hazy crowd. 'We fished her out of the water. I think she needs a new nappy.' I couldn't see anyone clearly, but I knew DD wasn't far away.

'Goggles!' she yelled. 'He saved her. And he saved Nig. He's a hero. He's just like...'

'Shut up,' I hissed. 'I'm not like anyone. I'm me, that's all.' I held out the wriggling bundle. 'Does anyone recognize her? The dressing gown was pink before it got dirty, and it's got an 'H' on the front.'

'Harriet,' sobbed the woman. She sounded very young and frightened. 'It's our Harriet. Thank God she's safe.' She took the little girl from me and cuddled her tightly. Then she said, 'Did you see anyone else? A young woman? Or a soldier with his arm in a sling?'

I shook my head. 'Not since the flood. Everyone ran the other way and we lost them. And then one of the archways got sealed up. I think some people must have escaped up the back stairs, but no one else came down the tunnel with us. I'm sorry.'

She backed away slowly. 'Thank you,' she said, in the saddest voice I'd ever heard. 'Thank you anyway.'

I didn't know what to say. I stood like a statue, afraid to move in case I started crying as well. I fumbled around for my glasses, but I couldn't remember where I'd put them.

'Here they are,' said DD, plonking them on my nose. 'They were in your jacket. And I don't care what you say. When you came out of the tunnel, you looked just like Superman.'

'Yeah,' said Nig. 'You did a bit. With the rescued baby and everything.'

'Well, not any more,' I said crossly. 'Because I'm never going to take my goggles off again.' Then I saw their faces. DD's cheesy grin and Nig's red ears. My lips started to quiver, and my shoulders started to jump up and down. 'Just like Superman,' I giggled. 'Super-Goggles, you mean. Pow! Bam! Kerr-unch!'

'Super- Goggles,' they spluttered. 'Hee, hee, hee! Super-Goggles!'

We were lying on the rough grass by the side of the rails now, rolling about and holding our sides in agony. Everyone stared at us as though we'd gone mad, and perhaps we had for a moment. It must have been the relief, I suppose. But after a while we calmed down and flopped back, exhausted.

'What's that horrible whining noise?' asked DD. 'It's going on and on.'

'The all-clear siren, I think,' I said. 'It means the air raid's over, so there won't be any more bombs tonight.' The sky was peppered with stars, and there was a deep red glow, as if the sun had decided to rise in the middle of the night. But it wasn't the sun. It was fire. Half of London must have been burning.

There were crowds of people rushing down the slope of the embankment, all carrying shovels or pickaxes or coils of rubber piping. A man in a peaked cap was shouting for ropes, and someone else was asking for a water pump.

'That must be the Ghost Train,' I said, pointing at the dark shape of an engine, still and silent against the night sky, like a sleeping dragon. 'It's the one Figgsy told us about. I think my Gran used to go to work on one of those, before she gave up being a Fluffer.'

'Yeah,' said Pam, thudding down beside us with Nosy and Mandy. 'And I bet all those women are engineers. I'm gonna be a plumber when I grow up.'

'I'm not,' said Mandy, who was juggling with three small stones. 'I'm going to be the first lady boss of the Magic Circle.'

'I thought you were going to be a pickpocket,' I said,

and in my mind I suddenly saw a busy platform full of jostling tourists. I sat up with such a jolt that she lost her rhythm and dropped the stones. 'Serves you right,' I told her. 'All those cameras and watches you stole must have got ruined.'

'Didn't take any cameras and watches,' she answered in her snooty way. 'Never do.' And we all watched in amazement as she reached into her pockets and pulled out a collection of crumpled sweet wrappers, used bus tickets and empty film cartons.

'What happened to all the loot?' Nosy asked. He sounded really disappointed.

'Must have lost it all when the water swept us away,' said Pam.

'No I didn't.' Mandy gave us another of her slow winks. 'I put all the valuable stuff back. I always do. I don't want to be a thief. I'm only practising for my stage act at the end of term show.' Then with a professional flick of her wrist she aimed a pellet of squishy paper in my direction.

When I unrolled it, I gasped out loud. 'It's Mum's shopping list. How did you do that? It was folded up with her money.' I checked inside the front of my jacket, and there was the purse, zipped tightly shut. So I opened it and counted everything twice. Not a single penny was missing.

'That's incredible. You're a genius...' I started to say, but Mandy just laughed.

'My father taught me,' she said, trying four stones this time. 'He's good at stuff like that. He borrows watches and smashes them up with mallets, then he pulls them out of a coconut and they're perfectly all right again. He sets fire to five pound notes as well. Want to see?'

'No thanks,' I said, putting the purse away quickly. 'What else can you do?'

'Well. I've been learning a trick where you ask

someone to come up on stage, and while you're talking to him you steal his braces. You have to do it really sneakily so he doesn't guess. Then he goes back to his seat and his trousers fall down.' Mandy stopped juggling and leaned closer. 'But I really need an assistant, because it's a lot harder than it looks. Any offers?'

'Not likely,' said Nig, pulling his anorak over his knees. 'I don't wear braces.'

'Nosy does,' giggled Pam. 'He's got an old pair in the wardrobe. I've seen them. I can get them for you if you...'

'No you can't.' Nosy stared down at his soaked jeans. 'Because we haven't got a wardrobe any more. We haven't even got a home. Have we?'

We all wriggled uncomfortably. It was the thought we had all been trying to forget. We were safe, and we were alive. But where were we? And how were we ever going to find our way back to our own time?

'Not the tunnel again,' moaned Nig. 'I can't face it.'

I gazed across at the mounds of earth and bricks. People were swarming round the hole they had cleared, and the hoses were being inspected for damage.

'We can't go back that way,' I said. 'The flood must have broken through by now. We'll have to think of something else.' But my brain was empty. I tried to remember what Mum and Jackie looked like. I tried desperately to picture Auntie Hat and Gran. Nothing. Just shadows and unfinished jigsaws.

'Thank you again,' said a sad voice. 'I'm taking her home now. She needs a warm bath and something to eat. I'll never forget what you did. If you hadn't been here, goodness knows what would have happened to her.'

I looked up. It was the young woman, with Baby H. The little girl was grizzling softly now, but she had been wrapped in a thick cardigan and had stopped shivering.

'That's OK,' I began. 'We all helped. Mandy carried her most of the way, and...'

My throat went dry. I couldn't think of anything else to say. I just kept staring at the woman. She was wearing a uniform of some sort, with metal buttons that gleamed softly in the moonlight, and her face was very young. It would have been pretty if she had been smiling. And I knew where I had seen it before - the photo inside my topic folder, somewhere far away in another world.

The woman turned away and two of the other engineers helped her up the steep slope to the embankment fence.

'Let's go,' I said, standing up.

'Where?' DD jumped up to join me. Honestly, I think she'd have swum all the way back to the station if I'd asked her.

'This way,' I said. I dug my hands in my pockets and began to squelch up the grassy bank in a zigzag path. The others followed us, and as we reached the top a gang of men came past us with a heavy rope.

'I'll go first,' one of them was saying. 'Down the Fluffers' route. I'll lead the way.'

'Forget it, Jack,' said the American. 'You've done enough. Let someone else take the risk.'

But the first man shook his head and limped off down the slope.

'It's the man in the blue cap,' said DD. 'The one we tripped over when we fell through the archway.'

He swung round to peer at us. 'Oi,' he said. 'You kids. How bad was the flooding in the tunnel? Can we get back to the platform?'

'I'm not sure,' I called down to him. 'The water was really fierce and it'll be much deeper by now.'

The man nodded. 'Well. We've still got to try, haven't we? Anything's better than not trying at all.' He moved off, then paused and looked back over his shoulder.

'You're a Parker, aren't you?' he said to Nosy. 'Your Mum's going to skin you when you get home.'

'If I get home,' muttered Nosy. 'Come on Goggles. Get us out of here.'

I nodded. I didn't know where I was going or what I was doing, but the man in the blue cap had been right. Anything was better than not trying at all. 'This way,' I said again. I darted past the wide gap that the rescue party had made and edged along a narrow path next to the wooden fencing. A large white notice had been nailed to a post, and I could guess what it said. 'Keep Off. Trespassers Will Be Prosecuted.'

'Hang on. Wait for me,' panted Nig. 'I'll tell you what. If we ever get back to the garages, I'm never going to smoke again. My chest's thumping like a steam engine. How much further have we got to go?'

'Just along here,' I said. 'I'm sure it's just along here.' I was pressing each slat of wood as I skidded by, and I was just beginning to give up hope when I felt myself lurch sideways.

'This is it,' I shouted. 'I'm sure this is it. Well, almost sure, anyway.'

The piece of loose fencing tilted, and I dived through the gap. Only, this was the slowest dive I had ever known. It was like dropping to the bottom of the world's deepest lake, and it seemed to take hours before I finally started to rise to the top again.

But the weirdest thing of all was that I felt very, very warm and dry. I was in a huge, swirling tumble-drier. And by the time I reached the surface I felt as if I'd been rolled in a thousand fluffy towels. Every single bit of me was clean and glowing.

'We're home!' I yelled. 'All clear! Hurry up, everyone. We're home!'

10
Bombshell

'How can you be so sure?' asked Nig, blundering through the fence behind me.

I rumpled my hair with my fingers. 'I don't know,' I said. 'But it feels different. And the sun's shining. And I can't hear the sirens any more.'

'Look at all that junk,' said DD. 'Did people have supermarket trolleys in those days?'

We were standing in a familiar alleyway, littered with empty drink cans and beefburger boxes. A rusty trolley was lying on its side, and an enormous cat was asleep between its handles.

'My hair's not wet,' said Pam. 'I've been trying to wring it out, and I can't get one little drip.'

'There's a couple of little drips right here,' Nosy started to say, but he stopped when he saw the look Mandy was giving him.

'That was a brilliant trick, Goggles,' she said. 'Better than any of the magic I can do. D'you think we could get back again if we went through the same gap?'

'Dunno,' I said. 'I suppose we could try.'

I wasn't at all keen. I reckoned I'd taken enough chances for one day. But Nosy was already shoving his way through the loose fencing, so we all crowded round and peered down at the shining railway tracks. There was no Ghost Train, no rescue party, no ruined tunnel, no buckled line. Just the usual rough grass and rubble...

'Oi!' shouted a cracked voice. 'You kids! Clear off home! Bloomin' vandals. Bloomin' trespassers. I blame the bloomin' teachers.' It was Jack the Lad, wearing his old blue cap. He held a black plastic sack in one hand and a metal grabber in the other. 'Dropping litter on my embankment,' he grumbled on. 'Looking for trouble. I blame the bloomin' parents.'

He attacked a crisp bag with the pincers and dropped it in his bag. Then he looked up and peered at us more closely. 'Seen you lot before,' he said. 'You're a Parker aren't you?' Nosy drew back, covering his nose with a hanky. It seemed to be DD's, but all the blood stains had gone.

'We were at the station,' I said. 'Last week. You took us round to look at the signals and everything.' I was feeling a bit sweaty now, and Nosy looked as if he was going to be sick.

'Maybe,' said Jack. He stared at us hard and long, then he shook his head. 'Bloomin' kids,' he muttered. But his voice was more friendly now, and his mouth suddenly stretched itself into a wide, white smile. We all relaxed, and Nosy passed the hanky back to DD.

'We could come and help you sometimes, if you like,' said Nig. 'We like clearing things up, don't we Goggles?'

'Yep,' I said. 'We're good at it.' But Jack didn't answer. He just kept smiling at us, as if his teeth had got stuck together, so DD waved her hanky at him and we ducked our heads back under the fencing.

'He knew we were at the flood, didn't he?' panted DD as we raced away down the alley. 'Because he was there too, and he remembered our faces.'

'Yeah,' said Nosy. 'And my rotten nose. I'm fed up with it.'

We swerved round the corner and tried to look natural as we dodged into the main street. Even DD

102

walked normally for a change.

'What's wrong with the station?' asked Pam. 'Why are all those people crowding round the front?'

A siren wailed, and an ambulance hurtled past us. For one horrible moment I though we must have slipped back through time into the middle of another air raid, but then I saw Figgsy standing on the pavement and I knew we must be all right. He was looking rather agitated in his battered slippers, and surprisingly small without his high stool.

'Oh dear, oh dear,' he said when he saw us. 'I hope you don't want to ask me a lot of questions. I'm afraid I've got a bit of a crisis on my hands.'

Two ambulance men charged past him carrying a folded stretcher and disappeared through the main entrance, while the crowd shuffled excitedly. The air buzzed with messy rumours. 'Blood everywhere. Dead bodies. Terrible tragedy. Shouldn't be allowed.'

'That's a good way to get in for free,' said Nosy. 'Perhaps I'll drive an ambulance when I grow up.'

'What's happened?' I asked. 'Has somebody been hurt?'

Figgsy mopped his head with a dishcloth. 'Don't know yet. Not till we shift the scaffolding. Apparently the workmen caught some kids messing about in the walkway, and the whole lot collapsed. Oh dear, oh dear.'

I blinked round at the others. Nosy was studying a pigeon on a nearby rooftop, and the girls were busily adjusting their socks. Nig had discovered a fascinating bus ticket in his pocket.

'How many kids?' I asked innocently. 'Boys or girls?'

Figgsy shrugged forlornly. 'No one seems to know. It all happened so fast. The men didn't even get a good look at them before the poles slipped.'

'Oh,' I said. 'What a shame.'

'Yeah,' murmured the others. 'What a shame.'

We began to edge away, but as we did so the ambulance men burst out of the station again, still carrying their folded stretcher. They looked slightly annoyed, and they were being followed by a couple of arm-waving workmen in dusty dungarees.

'Sorry, boys,' the first one was saying. 'Can't understand it. Definitely saw them, didn't we Baz? Just before the planks slipped.'

'That's right,' said the second. 'Can't see how on earth they got out. Not unless they were ghosts. Not unless they walked through the wall.' He finished with a nervous laugh and buried his hands under his armpits.

'Or unless you were seeing things,' muttered the ambulance driver, as he climbed back into his seat. 'You must have spent a bit too long in the pub this morning. I should stick to tea in future.' The engine roared into life, and the crowd drifted away, mumbling with disappointment.

'Thank goodness for that,' said Figgsy. 'Back to work, lads. I want everything straight before next week. And if you've got time, I need someone to fix a chewing gum machine.'

The workmen staggered off still waving their arms, and Figgsy headed back to his office. A queue was already forming for tickets, and several people were complaining in foreign languages.

'Um, excuse me,' called Nosy, chasing after the little man. 'I think these might be yours. Some kids ran past us and dropped them, so we brought them back.' And before Figgsy could say anything, Nosy presented him with a handful of unopened chewing gum packets. Then we all scooted away and leaned our backs against a newspaper stand.

'Why did you do that?' I asked Nosy.

He shrugged. 'Dunno. Just felt like it. Seemed the

right thing to do.' His stomach rumbled loudly and he wrinkled his nose. 'Should've eaten them,' he said. 'What's the time? I'm starving.'

Nig looked at his watch and shook it hard. 'Twelve fifteen. Lousy thing's not working. The water must've stopped it.'

'No it didn't,' said DD. 'Look.' On the other side of the road was an electrical shop, and above the door we could see a digital display. Twelve thirteen. Twelve fourteen.

'I can't believe it,' I said. 'We were only away for about ten minutes. That's impossible.'

'No it's not,' said Mandy. 'Nothing's impossible. You ask my father.'

'So long as you don't ask mine,' said Nig. 'His horse race starts at twelve thirty, and he's bound to lose. He always does.'

Someone was hurrying down the street towards us, and we swung round to see who it was. Had Figgsy decided to come after us? Or the workmen?

'Gran!' I yelled. 'What are you doing here?' She usually kept well away from the station, and would cross the road rather than walk anywhere near it.

'Oh,' she said, all flustered and frizzy. 'You're here. You're all right. I heard the ambulance and I thought something was happening at the station. I thought...'

'It was a false alarm,' I said. 'Everything's OK now. Honestly.'

'Oh.' Gran seemed confused. 'No one hurt? No bomb scares? No accidents in the walkways?'

We shook our heads. What else could we do?

'I can't understand it,' she said. 'I was so sure...' Then she stopped. She had finally noticed the Garage Gang.

'You've seen DD before,' I said, starting my introduction routine. 'And this is Nig. He came home with me once.'

'Yes,' she said softly. 'I remember.' She looked him up and down. 'You'll do,' she was murmuring. 'You'll do.'

I moved on to Pam and Nosy. 'And these are...'

'Yes. Yes. I know a Parker when I see one.' Nosy tried to hide his nose with his hand, but Gran was smiling at Pam. 'You've got your Great Grandmother's eyes,' she said. 'A wonderful woman. Everyone liked her.'

'And Mandy,' I went on. 'She's...'

'She's got clever hands,' Gran finished for me. Her eyes looked rather odd and misty, and she was inspecting Mandy's palms like a seaside fortune teller. 'Kind hands too. She'll grow up to be someone very special. Very special indeed.'

Nosy's stomach rumbled again, and we all laughed. 'I'm going,' he said. 'I'm ready for a plate of beans.' He gave us all a friendly wave and set off down the street with Pam.

'You see,' I said. 'There was nothing to worry about. We're all fine.'

'Hmmm.' Gran watched the twins go with a puzzled frown. 'All the same, the dream I had last night was so vivid. There were miles of dark tunnels and I knew your friend was afraid, but every time I tried to find him, someone started shouting, 'Bombshell! Bombshell!' over and over again. I still can't understand how I could have been so wrong.'

'Bombshell?' shouted Nig. 'Did you say Bombshell? That's the name of my Dad's horse. Blond Bombshell. Gawd! Don't say it's won.' Then he was sprinting away in his big boots, towards his own row of terraced houses.

'I'll see you on Monday,' I called after him. 'Can't make it tomorrow. Sorry. I'm going out with my Dad.' And just for once, I really was sorry about missing the gang, but I don't think he heard me. He was too busy shouting, 'Bombshell! Blond Bombshell!' at the top of his voice.

'I told you,' said Mandy. 'Nothing's impossible.' She gave Gran a big hug, then ran off after Nig with a trail of flags spilling out of her top pocket.

Gran tucked me under one arm and DD under the other, and together we strolled home along the bustling pavement. There were a thousand things I wanted to ask, but I couldn't think where to start. In the end, it was DD who broke the spell.

'Goggles says you used to ride on the Ghost Train,' she said shyly. 'He says you used to work at the station. Is that true?'

I was afraid Gran would storm off in a temper, but she didn't. 'Yes,' she said. 'It's true. But something happened exactly fifty years ago today, and I've never gone down there since.' She stopped walking, and we all stood in front of a shop window. It was full of flowers.

'I wasn't afraid,' she went on. 'I didn't mind the darkness or the tunnels. After all, I used to be a Fluffer just like your Mum.'

DD and I nodded. We didn't dare to interrupt.

Gran took a deep breath. 'Then one night I had a terrible dream. I was in an underground shelter and I could hear bombs exploding outside. All around me people were screaming and panicking, and I couldn't breathe properly. I felt as if I was drowning. So the next day I warned everyone I knew. 'Don't go down the Tube tonight,' I said. 'Please find somewhere else to shelter.' But of course, most of them just laughed. Even my big sister.'

She stared through the glass at a bunch of paper daisies, then she began again. 'She was married before the war, but her husband had been killed in France so she lived on her own with her baby. A little girl called Harriet. Hatty for short. It was my evening off, and I was supposed to be visiting them, but at the last minute I had to go and help the Red Cross instead. I couldn't refuse, could I? The raids were terrible that night.'

She sniffed and blew her nose into a ridiculously small tissue. 'By the time I got back, it was too late. My sister had taken the baby and run to the Underground as soon as the siren sounded. A bomb landed right on the station and a water main burst. People were trapped in the walkways. It was a nightmare. Some of them got out. Old Jack was near the surface and he managed to escape, but another man went back to help the others. A soldier with a wounded arm. Then there was another blast and the roof caved in.'

The three of us stood quietly gazing at our own reflections amongst the roses and carnations. Somewhere behind Gran's old eyes, the pretty young woman looked out.

'The front of the station was completely blocked, so everyone tried the embankment. The work party was there, with the Ghost Train, so at least there was plenty of help. But no one could save my sister. Or the soldier. They were stuck in the walkway, you see.'

'But someone found little Harriet,' I said.

'Yes.' Gran gave my hand a squeeze. 'Your Auntie Hat. Some children rescued her, but they ran off before anyone remembered to ask their names. Jack thought they might be Parkers, but that was a mistake. Mrs Parker was the only person who listened to me. She kept her whole family squashed together in the shelter under the kitchen table. None of them went anywhere near the station that night.'

'Was the baby all right?' asked DD. 'She didn't catch a cold did she?'

Gran laughed and moved away from the flower shop. 'She certainly did. And nappy rash. But she got over it, and when I married Grandad we brought her up as our daughter. We had our own little girl a few years later, and the two of them were just like sisters.'

I nodded. Now I understood why Auntie Hat looked so different from my Mum. 'But why do you still stay away from the Underground, Gran?' I asked. 'I mean, there isn't going to be a Blitz or a flood now, is there?'

'No.' Gran sighed, but she kept on walking. 'I know that. But every time I see the station, I remember. And I feel so guilty. I should have been with my sister. I should have stopped her. I should have kept her safe.'

'But it wasn't your fault, Gran,' I said. 'You mustn't blame yourself. Even if you'd really bullied your sister, she still might not have listened. And what if you hadn't helped the Red Cross? What if you'd gone inside the shelter too? Baby Harriet wouldn't have had anyone to care for her, would she?'

'Mmm.' Gran sighed again. 'I know you're right. Perhaps it's time I tried to forgive myself. After all, it's been fifty years.'

'What about Jack the Lad?' asked DD. 'He's just the opposite. He can't stay away from the station.'

Gran laughed. 'That's true. And it's because he feels guilty too. He thinks he should have gone back with the wounded soldier, but he lost his nerve. And later, when he went back down the flooded tunnel, there was no one left to save. The passageway was completely demolished, and no one had the heart to rebuild it. They just bricked it up and left it as it was. But Jack was a real hero that night. When it was all over, his workmates noticed that he was dragging his leg. He'd been rushing around for hours with a broken ankle, and it's never mended properly. He still limps, even now. But he won't stop working. He says he has to take care of everything. Keep it looking nice, in memory of the people who died.'

'Well,' I said. 'It'll soon look lovely. They're putting

109

up new tiles in all the passageways.'

'Good,' said Gran. 'It's time. It's high time.' And she began to walk faster. We were all starving by now.

'I'd love to meet your Auntie Hat one day,' said DD, as we reached our front door. 'After hearing so much about her and everything.'

'Then you shall,' said Gran. 'She's coming to tea on Sunday, and I'm sure we can find room at the table for a little one like you.'

'Definitely,' I said. 'After all, DD's my best friend, you know.' And we watched her skip merrily backwards down the street, waving her hanky at us all the way. Don't ask me where she got her energy from. I felt as floppy as Figgsy's dishcloth.

'What's for lunch, Mum?' I shouted as soon as we got indoors.

'You should know,' said Mum. 'You did the shopping for me. Didn't you?'

I hadn't of course. So lunch was very late that day, and as soon as it was over I fell asleep on the settee. I didn't wake up until I heard a TV commentator shouting, 'Blond Bombshell!' and I opened my eyes to see an action replay of a sandy horse winning the big race by the tip of its nose.

It was dark already, and Mum was upstairs getting ready for work.

'Aren't you going to stop her, Gran?' I asked in a yawny voice. 'If today's so unlucky.'

She shook her head. Her hair didn't look frizzy any more, and she seemed unusually calm. 'No,' she said. 'It's all over now. All clear. Believe me.'

And I did.

There isn't much more to tell. The Garage Gang went on meeting every Saturday, but we didn't look for trouble any more, we looked for fun instead. It wasn't quite as exciting, but on the other hand, it wasn't half as exhausting either. And it was a lot more interesting than sitting around smoking.

Nig managed to pass his first swimming test, and by the end of the season we were all picked to swim in the local gala. Most of us in the freestyle relays, and Nig in the beginners' race. DD was our cheer-leader, and she told all the other schools that I'd got my scar when I rescued Auntie Hat from a runaway train. We didn't win any medals, but we all had a good time. And Mandy's conjuring tricks at the end-of-term concert stole the show, especially when she waved Nosy's braces in the air and his trousers fell down.

After the workmen had finished decorating the station, Jack the Lad finally let Figgsy give him a retirement party. He said it was about time somebody else kept the place in order, especially now the walls were so easy to clean. But he still carried on with his anti-litter campaign, and we often used to give him a hand at the weekends, or if we had a day off from school. He seemed to quite enjoy our company, even though he always called us 'those bloomin' kids'.

And my sister won her fashion award, thanks to good old Gran. The judges said they had never seen such an original and daring collection, and Jackie ended up modelling her own design on the cat-walk. We all wanted to watch her, of course, so Gran went for her first Tube ride in fifty years. It was worth it too, if only to see Jackie in a pair of floppy green dungarees.

'The Fluffer Look,' announced the compère proudly, and we all cheered.

As for my Dad, he did eventually turn up for our once-a-month meeting. He handed Mum a roll of money, then he grinned at me.

'Sorry I had to let you down last week, son,' he said.

'But I'll make it up to you. I've planned a special treat. How about a nice visit to the Transport Museum? We can have a good look at all the old buses and trams and tube trains...'

'No thanks, Dad,' I said. 'If you don't mind, I'd rather go to see the dinosaurs.' So that's what we did. Except that we took DD along with us, and it was the best outing we'd had for ages. Better still, when we got home, Mum had hired DD's favourite video for a surprise, and she even let Dad stay to watch it with us. I bet you can guess what the title of the film was, can't you? And you know, I do look a little bit like Superman. Well, when he's wearing his glasses, anyway.

So that's about all. Only, there's just one thing I still don't quite understand.

You see, when we jumped forward in time and found ourselves in the alley-way, everything was back to normal. We were all perfectly warm and dry, just as if nothing had happened. Even DD's hanky was clean.

So why was it that when I gave Mum her purse that Friday lunchtime, the money was as good as new, but her shopping list was still dripping wet?